FALCON'S FURY

For John Turner and the rest of the Shropshire
Peregrine Watch team, and also for Osian,
who read it first

The Czech Mate Mysteries: Falcon's Fury copyright © Frances Lincoln Limited 2008
Text copyright © Andrew Fusek Peters and Polly Peters 2008
Illustrations copyright © Naomi Tipping 2008

First published in Great Britain in 2008 by
Frances Lincoln Children's Books, 4 Torriano Mews,
Torriano Avenue, London NW5 2RZ
www.franceslincoln.com

British Library Cataloguing in Publication Data available on request

ISBN: 978-1-84507-634-4

Set in Times Ten CE

Printed in Singapore

1 3 5 7 9 8 6 4 2

Andrew Fusek Peters
Polly Peters

FALCON'S FURY

Illustrated
by Naomi Tipping

F

FRANCES LINCOLN
CHILDREN'S BOOKS

Contents

A very close shave

"Look out!" Jan shouted.

Marie swung round. "What…?" She turned to her brother and froze. He was hunched down, staring up into the grey sky.

"Don't move," he hissed, as she stepped instinctively back.

It plummeted straight towards them. The two children stared helplessly, as something hurtled down like a meteorite.

Marie held her breath. Briefly she saw streamlined, brown feathers with wings pulled back and a pair of huge eyes, boot-black shiny each side of a hooked beak. There was no time to be scared, to scream, no time even to turn.

Jan closed his eyes. But Marie just stared.

At the last moment its wings flared out, acting as brakes. The bird slammed into the branches of the tree they were standing under.

Marie blinked. "Oh!" she gasped. With a flurry of feathers and a screech the bird flapped off again, ungainly now, with the weight of a bloodied woodpigeon clutched in its sharp claws. The pigeon's head lolled as the hawk struggled to gain height.

"Is it safe now?" Jan peered between his fingers to see the bird vanish in the woods ahead.

"You know, Jan, older brothers are supposed to *protect* little sisters."

Jan straightened up. "What do you mean? And how was I supposed to know that birdy there was only out for a small snack and not looking for a couple of scrawny kids to add to his pile of bones? In any case," – Jan scanned the sky above the woods – "we'd better be going."

Slowly, they headed off down the field. At the bottom, their boots sank into the mud, leaving little hollow pools.

"Who said it was a *he*, anyway?" Marie pouted.

"Yeah, yeah. I'm sure the females can be just as vicious as the males if my little sister is anything to go by."

"Hey. look!" Marie bent down to examine something on the ground. It glittered: a coin, maybe?

"Found some treasure? Tell me we're going to be rich!"

Marie gave him a withering look. "Only if the wrapper to a chocolate cream egg has suddenly become priceless!"

"*Oi*, you two!" a voice yelled.

They turned to look back at the tree. Standing under it was a tall man who seemed to have appeared out of nowhere. He paused, then strode towards them waving a stick.

"Come here!" the man snarled. "This is private land!" He wore green wellies and a country jacket. His face was so lined, it looked as if someone had taken a knife and chiselled out the contours. Marie stared, thinking his eyes looked far crueller than any bird's.

"Don't just stand there!" Jan grabbed his sister and dragged her toward the nearest stile.

"Where do you think you're off to, eh? You miserable trespassers!"

The man was surprisingly fast behind them, like a rabbit that knows every jink and turn in the landscape. Jan and Marie leapt the stile and bolted down the sunken green lane on the other side. The banks were too high to scramble up, so the only way was down.

Jan stole a glance behind them. The man was smiling as he gained on them but it wasn't a pleasant smile. And his stick didn't look as if it was just for walking, either. Ahead of them lay the iron gate, but Marie was out of breath and began to lag behind. Why am I the scrawny one? she thought, trying to push her legs harder. Her mother called her the little elf of the family, while her brother got all the admiring looks from the girls at Priestcastle Secondary. And now she was being chased by a madman ranting on about trespass.

Only a few more metres. Her throat was dry as paper. She turned round and backed towards the gate as the man slowed down, eyeing his trapped prey. Up close he was huge and thin like a giant scarecrow.

Jan was already on the other side of the gate, shouting, "Come on, Marie. Stop dithering!" But he was too late.

The man raised his stick, which was topped by a carved falcon's head, with the beak sharpened to a point. Then he shook it and drew a long breath.

"Mr Witherman!"

The stick dropped from his hand and his head snapped up in surprise. Lady Beddoes stomped towards the gate, taking in the whole scene.

Witherman's face fell and the dark eyes became hooded. He bent to retrieve his stick and pointed at the children. "These young vandals were trespassing on private property."

"As you are now trespassing on mine. I don't recall inviting you in. Nor do I see any young vandals, unless you mean this pair of delightful children. And I have no doubt they were enjoying an innocent walk until you spoiled it for them!"

Jan and Marie looked on in amazement. Lady Beddoes, in her muddy outdoor skirt, tatty tweed coat

and messy bird's-nest hair looked no match for the towering Witherman. But her voice held firm. "Good day to you, Mr Witherman."

Witherman glared and opened his mouth again, but thought better of it. Instead, he ground his teeth and nodded curtly at her. Then he swivelled on his heels and sloped off, grumbling under his breath with the stick now safely tucked under his arm.

"We weren't trespassing, Lady B! Honestly." Jan helped Marie climb over the gate. "I'm sure it was on a footpath. There was a stile…"

"Don't worry, children, I believe you. That man ought to be put away. How dare he!"

Marie was shaking. First the bird, now this.

Lady Beddoes glanced at her and quickly changed the subject. "Now your mother wants you to help with the schneetzels."

Marie managed a smile. "It's schnitzels for dinner, not shneetzels. You make it sound like fried sneezes!"

"Well, this Czech food is difficult to pronounce, but delicious to eat, and it's a joy to have you all staying, if only to take advantage of your wonderful mother! So, come along. You can show me how to make – *shintles!*"

Jan and Marie laughed. "Sch-n-it-zels!" they chorused. The thought of food cheered them enormously.

Back at the house, they were home and safe.

The whole family were the guests of Lady Beddoes of Bagbury Hall while their father was teaching Maths at Priestcastle High school for two years. For the Klečeks, it was a new beginning in a new country far from the Czech village of Valašské Klobouky.

Their new life in Shropshire had started off badly in cold, leaky Shoe Cottage but that house and the evil landlord Bob Thomson were now a distant memory. And it was thanks to the detective work of the two young Klečeks that Lady Beddoes was now restored to her rightful home. Bagbury Hall was quite a change for the family. With its columns by the grand front door and the huge, rectangular windows looking down an avenue of lime trees, it made Marie feel as if she had landed in a fairy tale.

"Now go in, you two, and take this with you." Lady Beddoes handed Marie a muddy plastic bag. "That's the last of the potatoes, grown out of my compost peelings – they'll be the best-tasting of the lot! And don't you worry about Witherman, you hear me?" She grabbed a garden fork and began digging the vegetable patch. "I'll be with you in a minute!"

Jan and Marie rushed into the boot-room, threw off their wet coats and boots and dived into the huge farmhouse kitchen. Their socks made damp footprints on the quarry-tiled floor.

"There you are!" said Eva Kleček as she fussed over the Aga stove. Her brown hair was scrunched up into an untidy bun and she wore an apron printed with pink teddy bears. Marie was glad no one else was around to see the embarrassing sight. "If you want to earn your dinner, wash those grubby hands and help me coat the schnitzels."

The pork steaks were laid out on the wooden butcher's block.

"Now, who wants to get violent?" asked Eva. Marie was only too happy to oblige. She grabbed the wooden mallet out of her mother's hands and began bashing the steaks viciously, all the while thinking of the man who had chased them. Jan pretended to back away.

"All right, Marie, you've made your point. I wouldn't want to be caught by you down a dark alley!"

The mallet had a waffle surface on the end, so, as she bashed, the steaks grew thinner and larger. Then it was Jan's turn to coat them in a mix of egg yolks and milk and finally dip them in a bowl of breadcrumbs, until they were ready for frying. Soon, aromas of cooking filled the room.

***

Lady Beddoes sat at the head of the table as the bowl of potato salad was passed round. The schnitzel steaks were crispy on the outside and juicy and tender inside.

"English potatoes and Czech recipes. It's a winning combination!"

Mrs Kleček beamed. As far as she was concerned, anyone who liked her food was a friend for life. Jan and Marie's father, František, wiped his moustache and sat back in the chair.

"After too many gruelling maths lessons, this *sums* up my day very nicely."

Everyone groaned. František was desperate to practise his English and had fallen in love with the British humour of puns.

Suddenly, Marie burst out crying. Everyone fell silent, looking at each other in surprise.

"Come on, Marie. Dad's jokes aren't that bad!" Jan joked.

"*Maruško! Co se stalo?*" Her mother rushed over, but Marie pushed her away. She shook her head and stayed silent.

Lady Beddoes sighed. "Unfortunately, your two children had a rather unpleasant encounter with our local gamekeeper."

"We were on a footpath. What laws did we break?" Jan said furiously.

"Only the unwritten law of protecting his master's land. And his employer is a very rich and powerful man. So it's probably best to avoid that route back from school for a while. Now then," said Lady B, once again deftly changing the subject. "Marie, help me pronounce the name of this delicious-looking pudding, will you?"

Later, as Marie was snuggling down to sleep in her bedroom, she could hear the wind rattling the window panes. That was the problem with Bagbury Hall. It was certainly magnificent, but it was also old. and being old meant it creaked and groaned just like an elderly pensioner. And every shifting noise sounded like footsteps, like a man with a stick striding along the passage.

Guardians of treasure

"Pass the marmalade," said Jan.

"There's a word missing!" Marie replied. She was irritable after a bad night's sleep.

Jan looked round the breakfast table. "Nope. Can't see it. It must have slipped off the edge…"

"Ha-ha! Looks like the jam is going to have to stay on my side."

"Will you two stop squabbling? I'm trying to read the paper." František gave a *harrumph* and shook the pages noisily.

"All right then, little sister. You win. Pass the marmalade, pleeeeease." Jan stretched the word to be annoying but Marie ignored him. "Anyway, *Táto*, this beats pork dripping."

František put his paper down. "On the contrary! Pork fat – spread thickly on rye bread, sprinkled with a few caraway seeds and some salt – what better way to start the day?" Jan and Marie made gagging sounds. Their father ignored them and pointed to the headline in front of him. "Ah! I do love the local paper. Front page news – someone *might* steal a bunch of eggs!

It makes me glad to be living in the countryside!"

Jan pulled the paper across the table and studied it. "I thought you were trying to read this! You haven't even looked at it properly. Here, listen!"

Residents in South Shropshire have been asked to be on the lookout for illegal egg thieves in the next two months. The mating season for Peregrine Falcons is under way and the females start laying from the beginning of April. Unfortunately, Peregrines are particularly vulnerable to egg theft and with only 16 pairs reported in Shropshire, it's an uncertain future for them.

A member of the local Peregrine Watch team told the Journal: "These nest robbers are not just criminal, they're barbaric. It's bad enough that certain farming practices, not to mention the actions of other unscrupulous types, have reduced British breeding pairs to 1,200, but then along come these 'collectors' who will stop at nothing to add to their collection. The underground trade in eggs and chicks is scandalous, with the black-market price of a Peregrine chick set at about £3,000. Of course, we try to keep the nesting sites secret, but these people are as obsessive as train-spotters and ruthless as sharks."

"There's a number to ring if anyone spots any suspicious activity." Jan put the paper down.

"Well, it's a sad world out there." František sighed. "Hope you two haven't got a secret collection of eggs under your bed!" Then he kissed them both on the forehead, struggled into his coat and straightened his tie, ready to head off for another day of teaching. "Are you coming with me, Jan?"

Jan didn't want to point out that turning up to school with his father was totally uncool, both in the Czech Republic and Shropshire. "I'll catch you up!"

"Okey dokey. Have a good day!"

The door slammed.

Marie leaned over Jan's shoulder. "Look at the picture!"

"So?"

"Yesterday, remember?"

Jan's face lit up: "The mad bird from hell."

"Exactly. Look at those eyes, that beak. It was a Peregrine! No surprise that they don't like us humans."

"Why? We didn't do anything."

"Don't be so stupid for once in your life, Jan." Marie frowned. "It's horrible. I hope no one tries to steal her eggs when she lays them."

"Yeah, suppose so. Come on, or we'll be late for school."

***

"All right, Elf-face?"

Marie's English was rapidly improving. She understood exactly that the smile on Cassie's face was the exact opposite of what she was saying.

"Met any goblins recently?" Cassie carried on in a hissing whisper.

"Only you. The poor goblins must feel bad you are on their team," hissed back Marie.

Cassie went red and Ashleigh, Marie's best friend, gave her the thumbs up.

"Now, class, I hope you've all remembered your packed lunches. The coach arrives in ten minutes." Mrs Evans beamed at Year 6 class of Priestcastle Primary.

Only another term and a bit and Marie would join Jan at the high school. The only problem was that Cassie would be there too. It was hard enough being in a new country and learning a new language without having her own, home-grown tormenter determined to hunt her out at every opportunity.

On the bus she sat next to Ashleigh.

"Is the Hegley girl giving you grief again?"

Marie frowned. "Vot is giving greef?"

"Sorry. I meant, is she giving you a hard time?"

"Hard time? Yes. But vot have I done to her?

"Nothing. Anyway, ignore her, she's not worth it. Did you see her showing off the label on her jeans? Apparently that little square of material means they cost £100 more than anything the rest of us are wearing. I hope she falls over in them!"

***

The bus soon pulled up at the edge of the castle. Marie was impressed. A huge, dry moat led to enormous stone walls rearing into the sky. Crows flew above the battlements, their raucous caws echoing over the valley.

Marie spotted her mother climbing out of their rusty old Škoda on the other side of the car park. Mrs Evans had asked for parent helpers on the visit. Just what Marie didn't need… and if Cassie spotted the car, then the Škoda jokes wouldn't be far behind.

Everyone piled inside the shadowy gatehouse, where a man waited to greet the class. He was old and slightly stooped as if to apologise for being so tall. His thinning white hair topped a knobbly face and nose that seemed moulded out of plasticine. But there was nothing soft about his sharp, keen eyes. He was leaning on a stick for support, a stick with a carved bird's head.

"Welcome to my house!" boomed the man, who suddenly didn't seem old at all. "Well, it's not my house, but I am its keeper! My name is Donald and I'm at your service. Now, follow me!" With that, he strode off surprisingly quickly, folding himself through the tiny door that led into the inner courtyard. When the whole class was assembled, he used his stick as a pointer.

"These walls, believe it or not, are just like your designer trainers!" He paused for a second. Cassie twirled her finger round her head to indicate exactly what she thought of this strange man. "Yes, there's always one young person who thinks I'm not all there!" Mrs Evans gave Cassie a threatening look. "But my point is this. Our local merchant, Laurence De Ludlow built this place using his profits from wool. Sheep were big business in those days. There were no wars going on at the time, but nevertheless, battlements were the latest thing to add to your house – a bit like pebble-dashing. They called it 'crenellation'. And I assure you, his neighbours were most impressed! After all, an Englishman's home is his castle…"

Marie liked this man. He brought the fusty old building to life, though she couldn't help glancing at his stick. Their guide scuttled off again, straight into the empty hall where the roof towered twenty metres

above them. He asked them to sit on the floor in a circle. The shutters to the high windows were closed, so the edges of the hall were lost in shadow.

"Imagine a huge fire pit in the middle of the floor: roasting pigs, feasting, musicians playing in the minstrels' gallery up there." He pointed to a high ledge jutting out precariously, "And after food and much wine, there were stories to be told. This is one of them." He paused to mop his face and Marie closed her eyes, imagining the play of flames on tapestry walls, the wild wind trying to push in from outside.

"There were two giants who lived on the hills on either side of this castle, and they were brothers. Now, who here has a brother or sister?" Nearly the whole class put their hands up. "And who here fights and bickers with them on a daily basis?" he asked with a glint in his eye. The hands stayed up. "Exactly. These two giants were no different. They kept their money and treasure locked in a box in this very hall. But there was a problem. There was only one key. And a single key can have only one keeper. So, each brother would take it in turns. If the other giant needed money, he would shout right across the valley and his brother would throw the key with all his might so that it flew like a falcon over the hills to land in the other's palm. But remember what I said about squabbling?" All the class nodded their heads. Even Cassie was entranced.

"Well, there came a day when they were having a right old ding-dong. One wanted the key, then the other. Backwards and forwards it went:

'It's my turn!'

'You've had it too long!'

'Give it back!'

'My stinking key!'

'No, it's not!'

They were like giant children squabbling, except that the sound of their tantrum was a hurricane.

Finally, the oldest of the two brothers flung the key angrily across the valley. It flew up into the clouds and then dropped like a stone – straight down with an almighty splash into the lake that lies just behind the castle. Of course, it was lost for ever."

The old man fell silent and stared at the floor.

Marie felt the spell break. It wasn't right, wasn't finished. "But vot about the treasure?"

"The treasure? Ah, yes. Well, the myth tells that a giant wild bird protects it: still there to this day. And as for the brothers, history is silent. No one knows."

The mood was broken. Children slowly began chatting as Donald handed a pile of activity sheets to the teacher, then shuffled away.

Marie couldn't contain herself any longer. She stood up and ducked through the door to catch up with the old man. The sudden daylight blinded her and she nearly tripped over him.

"Watch yourself, young lady. Are you looking for the toilets?"

"No. It's the story, the bird. Vich bird do you mean?"

"Curiosity… hmmm." He studied her for a second. "A good quality to have. Well, some say it's a raven. Others a peregrine. I know which one I would want to protect my treasure." He made to turn away again, but Marie stopped him with another question.

"My class is doing project on local wildlife at school. I saw a peregrine, I think, yesterday. It shot from the sky like – like shooting star!"

The man's eyes lit up. "That she would. What a beauty she is, eh?" Marie thought about this for a second, remembering how the bird had plunged into the tree. Yes, it was beautiful, dark and beautiful, though not for the pigeon.

"In a stoop – what you'd call a dive – she can reach speeds of up to two hundred miles an hour. Beats a sports car any day!" His face was animated as he spoke.

Mrs Kleček appeared in the doorway behind them and made her way over.

"*Maruško!*" she called.

"I deduce that this is your mother – am I right?"

Marie nodded. She would have to go back and do the activity sheets now.

"You said you were doing a project? Well, I might be able to help. I'm part of a local watch group and we monitor the birds' sites, try to give what protection we can. How do you fancy coming out with your family at the beginning of the holidays? We might even be able to see the female nesting."

Marie couldn't believe it. She quickly explained to her mother in Czech. Her mother scrutinised the old man. Then she smiled and nodded.

"Thank you for kind offer. Much thank you." She wrote the number of Bagbury Hall on a piece of paper and handed it to Donald with more thank-yous. Then she steered Marie back to tackle the worksheets.

Donald stood still, gripping his stick tightly. He absently scratched the head of the falcon as memories flew round him.

Trapped!

Mrs Evans stood in front of her class. "Can anyone tell me what facts they've found?"

The pupils were about to start a wall-display on the wildlife around Priestcastle.

Marie's hand shot up. "I have done some – vot is it? goggling – and the peregrine has eyes even bigger than humans. If ve had eyes that big, they vould only just fit inside our heads!"

Mrs Evans beamed. "Well done, Marie. It seems that your sharp eyes have done some of their own detective work!"

Marie was pleased, until she felt a sharp kick on the back of her legs. She flinched and turned round.

"Swot!" hissed Cassie.

"Did you say something, Cassie? I would love you to share it with the class." Mrs Evans was no fool, but as ever, Cassie slid easily out of trouble.

"Bad cough, miss." Next to her, a couple of her cronies smirked.

"I see." Mrs Evans frowned. "And tell me, where have your endeavours taken you?"

"Well…" Cassie scrunched her face up. "I've got it! Local birdlife: get a bunch of chickens in a shed. Sell the eggs and make tons of money! That's what my dad does!" She sat back and folded her arms.

"Really, Cassie! That's not exactly wildlife, is it?" Mrs Evans sounded exasperated. "Now, who would like to contribute something sensible?"

Marie felt her ears burning. What was wrong with being enthusiastic?

For the next hour, the class drew the various animals they had researched. Marie scribbled angrily, trying to capture the hooked beak and dark black eyes of the falcon. Others around her drew hares, buzzards, barn owls, mice and skylarks.

At break, Ashleigh sat with her on the wall at the edge of the playground. "She's just trying to wind you up, Marie."

Marie was puzzled. "Am I a ball of string?"

"No. It's… what I mean is, she's trying to get to you. Don't let her, right?" Ashleigh twirled her hair in her fingers. "Oh, message from my mum. She's put in a good word at the Poultry Palace for your brother."

Marie stared at her. She had no idea what Ashleigh was talking about. "But your mother is…"

"…A pain… I know! I have to live with her. But apparently, your mum bribed her with some of that fantastic poppy-seed cake of hers. And you know what a sweet tooth my mum has. Anyway, she reckons the holiday job is his."

"Votever…" Marie shrugged, pretending that whatever her brother did without telling her was of no interest to her.

Ashleigh looked at her watch. "Oh, recorder practice. Gotta go!" And she leaped off the wall and ran inside.

Sitting by herself, Marie was aware of being watched. A group of girls peeled away from the opposite side of the playground and sauntered towards her.

"It's the svot. Hello, svot! Ever heard of the letter *w*?" Cassie sneered. Her best friend Deanna and a couple of hangers-on laughed obligingly.

Marie went red. "This letter is not so easy to say in my language!" She wished she could think of a better response.

"Do we look like we care?" The gang crowded closer, almost pushing Marie off the wall.

"Oh, poor little Marie, better be careful – you wouldn't want to fall!" Cassie was enjoying every second, as she nudged Marie backwards.

"Vot are you doing?" Marie's voice rose.

The faces jeered at her, closing in. "Vot, vot, full of snot!"

One more second and she'd lose her balance.

Suddenly Cassie lunged towards her, determined to show her who was boss. But Marie slid smartly to one side, leaving an empty space where she had been sitting. Cassie toppled forwards and catapulted straight over the wall into a patch of nasty-looking nettles. Screams erupted and the playground helper, Miss Walcot came running over.

Cassie was in tears as red lumps welled up on her arms. She turned and pointed at Marie. "She pushed me, Miss!"

Though Deanna was usually rather slow on the uptake, she knew this was the time to join in.

"We saw her, Miss! She called Cassie all sorts of horrible things and then she pushed her over the wall!" It was a good story. The others were quick to agree.

Miss Walcot crooked her finger. "Right, you, over here!"

Marie couldn't believe it. Lies, all lies! But she was outnumbered. Cassie carried on wailing.

"Poor girl – run off to see Megan in the staff room – she'll sort you out with some sting cream. And as for you," Miss Walcot frowned at Marie. "The Head will want a serious explanation!"

Marie's only satisfaction was to see Cassie's expensive jeans covered in mud.

***

Jan felt as if there were an invisible force field around him. Wherever he went during school, Ross and his sister Kerry avoided him. If he walked down a corridor, he might as well have been covered in farmyard manure, the way they shrank back against the wall. Life was a lot better than last term, when the two had done their best to make his life a misery. It seemed that their parents, who were tenants of Lady B, were at last keeping a firm hand on their son and daughter. Jan enjoyed this new feeling of power. A couple of times he'd been tempted to jump out of a doorway at them,

just to see their reaction. But being left in peace was good enough for now.

Jan was in the changing rooms after football. The others had all gone when the door opened and in sauntered Doug. Doug was massive, built like a chip shop.

"All right, Jan?"

"Yes. It was a good game." Jan wasn't sure what else to say. After all, Doug had once been part of Ross and Kerry's gang, even though he'd turned round and done the right thing when things had gone beyond a joke.

"Heard about your run-in with Witherman."

"Really? How? Do you know him?"

"Everyone knows Witherman." Doug had his foot up on one of the changing benches. "Cousin heard him in the Five Bells, mouthing off." He paused to have a good chew on a fingernail. "Thing is, next time, your Lady B might not be around to protect you, if you know what I mean. This is a bloke who sets badger traps for fun. Watch yourself, eh?"

Jan couldn't work out if this was a threat or a friendly warning. Whose side was Doug on? But before he had a chance to ask, Doug decided the fingernail was well and truly nibbled.

He nodded at Jan and barged noisily out of the changing room.

The egg factory

"Are you going to help with the eggs, then?" It was the first day of the Easter holidays and Marie sat at the large kitchen table ready to start on the bowl of hard-boiled eggs.

Jan pulled on his coat. "Sorry, Marie. Some of us have got jobs to go to, and colouring eggs for Easter is not one of them." Jan's tone indicated that this particular Czech custom of dyeing eggs was now way beneath him. "Anyway, I am helping with eggs – I've got a holiday job at the Poultry Palace. Mr Hegley is taking me and Will on for 'general duties' – whatever that means. What it *does* mean, though, is money towards an Ipod!"

"Hegley?" Marie couldn't believe it. "Cassie's father?"

"Who? You mean that girl in your class?"

Marie nodded. She was lucky that the Head hadn't written home about the nettle incident. Instead, Marie had been made to chop down all the nettles and apologise to Cassie in front of the whole class. The thought of it still made her eyes sting with anger.

She'd wanted to tell Jan, but he'd been too busy hanging out with Will after school.

"Don't know, but he's certainly loaded. Owns half the property round here. And if he wants to pay me cash in hand at the end of each shift, who am I to say no? See you later."

And he was gone.

Mrs Kleček pulled out a box from the cupboard. Inside were little coloured tablets of dye and a packet of wax crayons. They both got to work. First the tablets were dropped into plastic cups filled with vinegar and boiling water. Then Marie drew a spiral all the way round her first egg. She dipped it into the bright orange cup, left it for a few minutes and then spooned it out into an empty egg box. The spiral shone out from an orange egg.

Soon they had several boxes full of brightly-coloured eggs, enough to fill a fruit bowl.

"These will keep for weeks now. See how pretty they look on the table!" Mrs Kleček looked across at Marie, who was still biting her bottom lip. "Your brother's growing up very quickly, Maruška. I can see… you've done the colouring together since you were little."

"I'm not bothered." Marie tried to focus on the eggs, but it wasn't working.

"Yes you are. There's no point trying to hide it. But listen, I've kept back the good news. That gentleman from Stokey Castle rang. He said that the peregrine has laid a clutch of eggs. He's invited us to visit the site tomorrow."

Marie looked up. "That sounds great. But what about Jan?"

"Listen to me, my girl. There is no way I'm letting him work on a Sunday. Let's start the holiday by seeing new life in the making!"

***

Jan pedalled hard down the lane, trying to avoid the pot-holes. The sky was in a good mood for a change, and the sun smiled cheerily. His friend Will turned up right on time.

"All right, Jan?"

"Hi, Will. Let's get set for Easter. How about an egg hunt?"

"You don't know what you've let yourself in for." Will tapped his nose as if he had founts of wisdom stuffed up there. They raced through the lanes away from Priestcastle and into the deep green Shropshire hills. Jan was glad that his mountain bike had eighteen gears as he puffed and panted to keep up with the sporty Will, whose long legs effortlessly pumped the pedals.

"Give me a chance, will you?

"What do you mean? We're here!" They both skidded to a halt and turned into the entrance. Ahead of them was the most enormous field Jan had ever seen, sloping gently towards the road. The far forest surrounding the farm was at least half a kilometre away. Whatever crop was growing, had only reached a few centimetres high. All the hedgerows had been grubbed up. It was green as far as the eye could see. A neat tarmac drive led right to the middle of the field where a cluster of sheds and buildings stood.

"Ugly, eh?"

Jan nodded. The whole place looked sterile, almost eerie.

"Come on then. Work to do, money to make!" Will raced ahead of him up the drive, until they found

themselves in the car park. Will noticed the huge shed on the left. He wrinkled his nose as a faint smell wafted towards him, sharp and acrid.

As they leaned their bikes against a wall, a man came out of a small door to the side of the shed. He closed the door carefully, locked it, then slipped the key into his pocket. As he turned, Jan saw that the man had a paper mask over his mouth and nose and was wearing thin rubber gloves. He spotted the boys and waved

them over, as he pulled off his blue overalls to reveal a smart suit underneath.

"You must be the new boys." He peeled the gloves off and leaned over to shake their hands. "Welcome to the Poultry Palace."

Jan noticed two things: one, his hair was shiny, as if glued in place and then polished; and two, he sported an extraordinary orange tan. The man looked like a baked potato with a set of teeth! However, his handshake was firm and friendly.

"I'm Rick Hegley and you must be Will and Jan." He even pronounced Jan's name right with a 'y' rather than a 'j'. "You're with me today, Jan, and Will can help Mr Whittaker with his duties." Will was led away by a man dressed in the same kind of overalls as the boss.

"Come on, then." Mr Hegley marched in the opposite direction without waiting, until they came to a Portakabin at the edge of the complex. "It's not much, but it's home. Get the kettle on, lad – I'm dying for a brew. Then I'll run you through the work."

The place was a mess. Piles of papers tottered on the old formica desk and the mug that Jan now stirred looked as if a bomb had gone off inside it. The walls were covered with pictures of different types of birds, including a framed painting of some chickens strutting around a farmyard, looking very chirpy. There was no way you could call this place a palace.

"Got loads of birds, I have!" He smiled at Jan.

Jan said nothing.

"Sorry. The oldest joke in the book. Of course, you're not from round here."

Jan suddenly remembered overhearing some of the boys at school talking about 'gorgeous-looking birds'. Mr Hegley was obviously trying to be funny and Jan was bright enough to work out that part of his job was to laugh at the boss's jokes, so politely he did his best.

The rest of the day passed in a blur of making cups of tea for the inordinately thirsty Mr Hegley, cycling into the nearest village to send some urgent post and hauling palettes of eggs into endless trucks. It was back-breaking dogsbody work, but the promise of cash at the end of the week and a dozen free eggs made it almost worthwhile.

"I never saw so many eggs in my life!" Will announced as they cycled away, "and the machinery was awesome, straight out of a horror movie. They've got these weird rubber clamps that suck the eggs up, fifty at a time, to plonk them on the trays. The whole place hums as if it's about to blow up, and we had to dress in this weird gear. Maybe they're worried we're going to catch something."

"It's called Bird Flu, Will! Anyway, what about the chickens?"

"Didn't see any. Only a conveyer belt with thousands of eggs on it."

Jan wondered for a second. The only chickens he had seen were in a painting on an office wall. Never mind. He was now on his way to an Ipod. And tomorrow was a day off.

A grim discovery

"I have far too much to do today!" Mrs Kleček looked frazzled as she rushed round. "*Janko*, it's no good. I just can't get away. Could you take your friend Will with you instead?"

Marie scowled, but she had no choice in the matter.

"And make sure you've got your wellies and hats!"

"Yes, Mum!" Jan and Marie chorused.

An hour later, the bell rang. Marie ran to open the big front door. Donald stood there, leaning on his stick.

"Are you ready?" he smiled. Marie stared. She nearly opened her mouth to say something, but stopped herself.

Donald caught her look. "It's a lovely bit of carving, eh? Anyway, hope you're all ready. She only laid last week, so you're in for a treat!"

Mrs Kleček rushed down the hall: "Ah, welcome, Mr Donald! So kind. And I'm so sorry... busy, busy today..." she flapped her flour-covered hands up and down. "Is possible to take Jan's friend instead? He is very nice boy."

Donald nodded, "No problem, Mrs Kleček.

All keen volunteers are welcome. So come along, you two."

Jan and Marie grabbed their coats and followed him outside. "See you later, Mum! We'll send your blessings to the birds!"

Donald's car was in an even worse state than the Klečeks' Škoda. It was filled with bits of paper, old apple rinds and empty juice cartons.

"You must excuse the mess in here. Sometimes I'm out all day on watch, and the car becomes a second home." Donald shook his head. "Yes, I could do with a vacuum cleaner in here. But there's no cupboard to put it in!"

The car coughed and spluttered its way down the drive and off through the lanes to pick up Will.

"You know how the peregrine got its name, don't you?" They had been in the car for fifteen minutes. Jan and Will were only half-listening, but Marie was fascinated. "It comes from the word *peregrination*, meaning 'to wander', and that's what our friend does – she wanders the sky. Now, here we are." Donald pulled into a lay-by, next to a barbed wire fence which said, "Private. Keep Out."

"The sign makes no difference. This old quarry attracts vandals like moths to a light."

Donald locked the car and they made their way in on foot. The gate was chained shut to stop joy-riders from carving up the landscape, but enterprising bikers had simply gone straight through the woods that surrounded the quarry. Marie could see their trails everywhere, scribbled in the mud under the trees.

"This is the old track that the trucks used to thunder along, bringing out the rock and hardcore."

They rounded a corner and the woods vanished. In front of them the landscape changed starkly. Huge grey mounds reared up into the sky, cut with fissures. Bits of rubbish floated in a dirty pool.

"Welcome to the peregrine's world!"

They turned a corner and the whole quarry opened up. It was like a giant's sandpit. Enormous stone walls veered up at crazy angles as they walked down into the huge crater, following the old track. Marie felt like an ant crawling around at the bottom of a prehistoric canyon.

"*Fantastický*!" said Jan.

"Yes, it is!" agreed Donald. His eyes scanned the rock surfaces. Crows and jackdaws wheeled round the site. "I can't hear them…"

"Hear vot?" asked Marie.

"Their call. It's very high, like a cat mewing, but… different. They don't leave the nest for long now that they've laid, so they should be around somewhere." Donald stopped in the middle of the track and began to set up his telescopic lens on a tripod. "Right. You see that wall over there, that juts out at 45 degrees?" He pointed straight ahead, about three hundred metres. "We mustn't disturb them. Just up there is the ledge where the female should be sitting. It's mostly the female that sits on the egg. But the tiercel helps out as well…"

"Vot is tiercel?" asked Marie.

"Another lovely word. The male peregrine is a third smaller than the female. Tiercel is from the Latin, meaning 'a third'."

Marie nudged Jan hard. "That's how it should be!" she hissed in Czech. "The female is the boss, and the little male does what he's told!"

Donald crouched down to peer into the lens. "Hmm. That's odd. Maybe my eyes aren't what they were. Could you have a look for me?"

Will bent over and peered through the telescope.

"All I can see is a ledge with a stick of gorse on it. No bird…"

"They do sometimes leave the nest, but never for long, or the jackdaws'll be in there." Donald looked worried. He scanned the quarry again. "Maybe we should take a closer look." He left the tripod and marched off ahead of them, almost running.

Within a minute, they were all standing under the rock face; a few metres of steep, muddy scree, and then the wall itself reared up. Marie realised it wasn't vertical at all and with a bit of scrambling and finding handholds, anybody could climb up there.

The silence was suddenly oppressive. Even the jackdaws had stopped their incessant chattering.

"Something's wrong."

Marie wandered towards the muddy slope while the others stared at the empty ledge above.

"Look!" she said. There were large indentations in the soil.

"It's mud, little sister. Mud with holes in it," said Jan. Will smirked too, which made Marie even angrier.

"No, stupid. They're footprints!"

Donald shook his head. "But there are no boot marks. It doesn't make sense."

"Yes it does. This earth is loose. I vill prove it!" She put one foot at the bottom of the scree, pressed hard and then stepped off. There was no footprint, just a loose hole where the boot had been. "And look, these holes have dry earth on surface, so they must have been made a day or more ago."

Jan was surprised "OK, I take it back. Brilliant detective work, *Maruška!*"

Marie ran up the slope until she came to the rock. "And the scrub has been pulled and broken here, which means…"

Everyone looked at each other. Donald sagged. "I came to show you the delights of nature. And this is what happens." He wiped his arm across his forehead.

"I do need to check this out properly, though, and the only way we can do that is to get up above the site. We daren't approach from below, in case the eggs are still there and we disturb the nest. Jan, come with me."

Marie desperately wanted to be part of the search party. She sat down sulkily at the top of the scree and looked round the quarry while Will went back to play with the telescope. Far away in the distance, a couple of teenagers rode their BMXs up and down the man-made slopes, screaming like animals. They were unlikely suspects, though. What would a couple of kids do with a clutch of rare eggs?

The sun came out from behind the grey clouds. One of the loose boot-prints glinted at her. She thought it might be a bit of glass or flint, but as she scrambled down, she saw it was a piece of scrunched-up foil –

silver on one side, coloured on the other. She paused for a second before slipping it in her pocket and moving over towards Will.

Jan followed Donald back down the track. They took a small winding path up through the brambles which finally doubled back on itself until they were standing on the lip of the quarry. Jan peered over the edge – the drop was at least twenty metres.

Donald came up, panting, behind him. "Damn. It's an overhang down there. We're going to have to get nearer." But barring their way was a steep slope covered with a jungle of thorny branches.

"There's no path!"

"We'll have to make one, then." Nothing was going to stop Donald. He laid into the brambles with his stick and slipped and slid his way down the slope. Jan tried to step carefully behind him, but his trousers were soon torn and blood trickled down into his socks from the scratches.

Finally, they reached a tiny foothold directly above the nest. One wrong step and they would plummet down.

"I still can't see!" Donald muttered. "Could you lean over?" He braced himself and held Jan's arm while Jan bent over the steep edge. Will and Marie stared up at him. How would the old man stop him falling? This was mad. Jan inched over and out into the void,

49

craning his head round the overhang, hoping to see the eggs. Suddenly his boots shifted. The sky began to spin and he slid over the edge.

"Aaaah! Pull me back!" he shouted.

"I'm trying!" grunted Donald, as his boots slithered on the loose earth. Jan's shoulder felt as if it was being slowly dislocated.

There was a sudden lurch… "Got you, my lad!" – and Jan fell back in a heap on the brambles.

Donald was shaking. "Thank the gods! Are you all right?"

"I think so!" panted Jan. "Bad news. There was… nothing there, except white-stained rock and… some gorse sticks."

Donald put his head in his hands. "What harm have they ever done us, eh? What harm have they ever done us?" He looked up with fury in his eyes. "If I found the man who did this, I'd kick him to kingdom come!"

Encounters and clues

Jan kept thinking about the empty nest. Donald was right. What harm had the peregrine ever done? As he walked into town the next morning, his ankles felt sore and scabbed from the brambles. He spotted Will cycling up the High Street.

"All right Jan? Cheer up. You look like the world's on top of you."

"*Ahoj,* Will! This whole egg business…"

"Yeah. It's pretty bad really. Are the police going to do anything?

"Donald said he'd report it. We might get interviewed."

"Cool! I fancy being interrogated under spotlights. Though if they tortured me, I might give the game away…"

"Ha-ha-ha!"

"Yes, I'm funny, I know. Thank you!" Will bowed to an imaginary audience. "Anyway, I'm not looking forward to work this afternoon. I've just been trying out something to distract me from the thought. Have you had a go on the new climbing wall in the gym?"

"So that's why you're wearing shorts in this freezing wind! Not trying to show off your knees to the girls?"

Will smiled. "If they saw my knees, they'd run a mile! I tell you what, though, you should've seen Doug the Thug. He was up and down that wall like a monkey. I never knew he had it in him. It's great fun, working out the handholds and everything. You should try it some time". Will glanced at his watch. "Oops, gotta go – see you at the farm?"

Jan nodded and waved absently as Will jumped back on his bike. He stood still, thinking hard. "Climbing... I wonder..." he murmured to himself.

***

Marie waited outside the supermarket for Jan to arrive. Standing around with several heavy plastic bags was not her idea of fun.

"Well, guess who?" a voice sneered, advancing along the pavement toward Marie.

It was Cassie

"Guess what? I know my own name!" Marie replied, turning away.

"Oh really. Think you're so clever?" Cassie stepped right in front of Marie and pushed her face up close. She was at least a head taller. Marie didn't move. She raised her eyes slowly,

"Better to be clever than stupid. Vot you think?"

Cassie paused, "I think it's time I introduced you to something that stings, so you know what it feels like!" She flicked back her long, brown hair like a whip while her other hand shot forward to grip Marie's arm so tightly, it hurt.

"But it vos your own fault! You tried to push me and then you lied!"

Cassie squeezed tighter and tugged Marie forwards. "That's your story! And now I hear your precious big brother has got a job at my dad's place. I don't like your family being round here, and I don't like you!" she hissed.

Marie dropped one of the bags. Oranges rolled away into the gutter. A couple of passers-by tutted but didn't intervene.

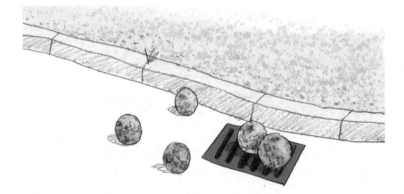

"Leave me alone!" Marie shouted.

"Hey! What's going on here?" Jan appeared round the corner.

Cassie turned and immediately dropped Marie's arm.

"Your sister and I were just having a little chat – isn't that right?"

Marie looked uncertain. She rubbed her arm.

Jan was furious. "A little chat? Pick those up!" He pointed at the oranges.

Cassie opened her mouth to protest, then shrugged. She was outnumbered. "Yeah, yeah! Whatever." She bent to pick up the fruit and threw it back into the plastic bag. "That's for Mummy's little helper!"

"If you weren't a girl, I'd…"

"What, Czech boy? Hit me! You haven't got the guts!" She stuck her tongue out and stalked away, smirking.

"Marie, what was all that about?"

Marie was close to tears. "That girl… every day in class she's been… I wanted to tell you but we don't seem to talk so much these days. Or you don't have time."

He sat her down on a wall. "That's unfair. I've been busy, that's all. Who is she?"

Marie told him in a rush: the bullying in class, the nettles, everything. "And now you're working for

55

her father. That's why I was so angry!"

"I'm not psychic! How should I have known? You never told me any of this!"

"Well, I have now." Marie wiped her nose on her sleeve. "It was my problem, and I wanted to sort it out my way."

"But I'm your brother – teamwork and all that?"

"Yes. I suppose so." She smiled.

"Good, we've got that straight. Now listen. About the eggs. Will said something…"

At that moment, someone stepped out of the shop door behind them with a mobile clamped to his ear. "Yeah. Yeah. Great. We'll check out the quarry again. Later." He snapped it shut and then spotted Will and Marie. He gave them a brief, uneasy nod and made to move away.

"Doug?" Jan stood up.

Doug turned round. "What?"

Jan took a deep breath. He was about to leap into the unknown: but it all fitted. "The quarry? So you like hanging out there – do you?"

Marie looked puzzled. What was Jan up to?

Doug's brow furrowed. "What's it to you, mate?" His massive shape loomed closer to Jan.

Jan gulped. Maybe this wasn't such a good idea. But what could Doug do out here in the open? He looked down at the pavement, "Will told me you were good at climbing."

"Are all the people from your country totally bonkers, or is it just you? Yeah, I'm into climbing. Is that a crime?"

Jan couldn't hold back now. "It was you, wasn't it?" He pointed a shaking finger at Doug's chest. "You stole the peregrine eggs!"

Doug exploded. He grabbed Jan by his sweatshirt and swept him up with one hand until Jan's feet were dangling. "I... don't... like... your... tone!"

"But..." Jan could barely speak. His face was burning.

Marie jumped up. First Cassie, and now Doug! It was too much

"Ow!" Doug let go suddenly, dropping Jan in a crumpled heap. He hopped round on one foot like a demented Morris dancer, holding the spot where Marie had just kicked him hard in the shin.

Marie helped Jan up off the pavement and strode up to Doug fearlessly. He towered above her.

"You leave my brother alone!"

Doug backed off under Marie's fierce stare. "He started it, right?" He continued rubbing his shin. "You've got a good aim, you have. D'you play football?"

Jan stood up slowly. "You still haven't answered… climbing… the quarry. It has to be you!"

"Now listen, you two. If someone is stupid enough to leave their wallet on a windowsill, then I'd be stupid to walk past it. But the peregrine? Well, respect where respect's due, I reckon. And I like climbing. So what? And I go quad-biking at the quarry. Doesn't make me a thief, does it?" Doug folded his arms and stared at them.

There was an uncomfortable silence, then he pulled a newspaper from his back pocket. "Says 'ere that they're gonna give fifteen hundred quid to whoever finds the bloke who did it. Strikes me as easy money."

Jan didn't want to believe Doug, but he sounded so convincing. "OK, OK. Sorry. So maybe I'm wrong, but tell me, when were you last at the quarry?"

"You don't give up, do you!" Doug rolled his eyes, then paused to think. "Last Saturday. Couple of mates – had a great time."

"But did you see anyone? Anyone else?"

Something flashed across Doug's face, but it was gone before either Jan or Marie noticed. "No. Nothing.

58

I mean, no one. Just us, having a laugh. And if I did see anything, why should I tell you? You'd get all the money!"

"Well… maybe we could share our information, share the reward!" Jan half-joked.

"Don't think so, mate. Nice try. And next time, keep that mad sister of yours away from me!"

With that, Doug turned abruptly and strolled away, limping slightly.

Jan stared after the retreating figure, wondering whether to believe him. He shook his head, then turned back to Marie.

"You were amazing!"

A man's house is his castle

Donald's house was hidden away down one of Priestcastle's many shuts – a series of shadowy, medieval alleyways that sliced up the town. Some of them simply led to back yards, while others ran along as single-storey passages with houses piled higgledy-piggledy above them. It was one of these that Marie and Jan were exploring the next day, trying to find the door with the bird's-beak knocker.

"This is it!" Marie said. The oak door had been weathered grey and the metal beak looked sharp enough to jab unwary strangers. The whole house appeared to lean forwards towards its neighbours, as if all those hundreds of years of standing upright had tired it out. Even the door-frame wasn't quite straight.

"Don't you think we'll be bothering him?"

"Not at all!" The door swung open and Donald looked down at them. "Visitors, especially enthusiastic ones, are always welcome. Don't dither on the doorstep! Come on in."

He swept them into the living-room, pierced here and there by shafts of light from the tiny, leaded windows. Marie peered around while Donald cleared some books from the sofa. It was a doll's house for the giant-sized Donald – a living-room, a tiny kitchenette and stairs leading upwards. The walls were covered in shelves of books: every single one was about birds.

"Cup of tea?"

Donald pottered round the kitchen, humming snatches of tunes to himself. Jan and Marie squeezed on to the sofa.

"It's not much!" said Donald, "But it's home. Being a guide for the Borders Trust won't ever make me a millionaire, but I'm happy here. Did you know that a hundred years ago, a whole family of hat-makers lived in this cottage? Ma and Pa and five kids. Amazing to think that in Broads on the High Street you could buy the latest fashions in hats, copied direct from Paris. We live in different times, eh?" He poured out tea from a chipped enamel pot and pushed a plate of chocolate biscuits towards them.

"It's a bad business, it is." Donald picked up one of his books on peregrines and opened it, passing it over to the children. "That's what we're looking for." He pointed to a picture of three eggs nestling precariously on a tiny rock ledge.

"But these eggs are…"

"Almost round – different from a chicken's egg. Often, the first one is pure white, like a pearl, but the others are rusty brown. You know the riddle, of course?" He leaned closer.

"Vot riddle?" Marie was curious.

"A-ha!" Donald spread his long arms expansively.

"A box with a hinge, without a lid,
Without any corners,
Filled with gold and silver..."

Jan took a bite of his biscuit and sipped the sweet, milky tea. "Umm..."

"Come, come: I've given it away already!" Donald's eyes glittered.

"Oh, I've got it!" Marie said suddenly. "The gold and silver is the precious treasure inside – like the story of the giants – yes? It's an egg!"

"Good girl! Jan, your sister has a brain on those shoulders of hers!" Donald paused. "And yes, they are precious, too precious to lose."

Jan's mind was on other things. "The local paper mentioned a reward. Maybe we could find the thieves?" He was still dreaming about an Ipod.

"Maybe you could. Who knows?" Donald stared off into the distance.

Marie noticed his stick resting in the corner. "I vonted to ask many times. That stick. Where does it come from? I have seen something like it."

Donald leaned back, surprised. "You have? Oh…" He paused and looked towards the stick, "Well now, there was once a carver, many years back: could see the life hidden in any old branch of yew or ash. With his knife, he could whittle wood until it almost breathed and… anyway, she's a beauty, isn't she?"

They both nodded. Marie didn't know if he was referring to the stick or the wooden falcon that reared up out of it. Something stopped her from mentioning Witherman. But the man who owned *this* stick was no threat. She wondered about the carver and why Donald's answer tailed off. Maybe it was a habit of his: he'd done the same thing at Stokey castle…

Donald refilled their mugs. "Heard about your job at Heg the Egg's."

"Who is Heg?" Jan looked confused.

"Sorry! Shropshire ways. We still call people by their jobs. I even have a secretive trout-fishing friend with the unfortunate nickname of Dave the Poach!" Donald smiled. "But Heg the Egg is Rick Hegley, who made his gigantic fortune through chicken eggs –

not that I approve. He's ploughed it back into property and land – a big estate, pheasants, woods, the lot. Plays at being the country gentleman."

Donald was about to say more, but the door-knocker clattered.

"Would you get that, Marie? My long legs have just got comfortable."

Marie rose and pulled open the door. "Oh, hello!"

PC Jim Cheever took off his hat and stooped inside the crooked doorway. "Good timing, I'd say. Mind if I come in, Donald?"

"Of course. Nice pot of tea on the go. And don't say as you won't, or I'll be insulted!"

"Well, it's been a long day- so yes, please. There's been a spate of wing mirrors pulled off cars on the High Street again. I'm sure I know the kids involved, but my superiors aren't about to go down the whole fingerprinting route." PC Cheever looked fed up.

There was no room for him to sit down, so he leaned against the shelves. "Thanks for reporting the egg theft."

Donald sighed, "You know the peregrine is a Schedule One protected species? The offence carries a jail sentence. The RSPB's newsletter Legal Eagle has just reported a case that resulted in imprisonment…" His voice was rising.

"I don't need the lecture, Don. We've been here

before. I feel as bad about this as you do. But without hard evidence, there's nothing we can do."

"But I found footprints!" Marie broke in.

"They were just holes in the mud," Jan replied.

PC Cheever carefully placed his tea on a pile of papers and pulled out his notebook. "Don told me you were both there – and your friend Will too."

They nodded.

"Can't do much with the footprints, unless there were identifiable indentations, I'm afraid."

"Big feet made them. I could tell." Marie explained, lifting her feet to demonstrate the difference in size.

"Well, I've got big feet," said Donald. "So have plenty of people."

"It's a start, though," the policeman admitted. "Did you see anything else?"

They both shook their heads. Jan's idea of detective work had been to accuse Doug, simply because of what Will had told him about the climbing wall, combined with his own eavesdropping .

"Look," said PC Cheever, "I've already opened a file on the case. We've had a couple of calls since the reward was offered but those leads went nowhere. I sometimes wonder if these rewards make any difference at all."

He finished his tea and stood up to leave.

"Perhaps the birds will mate again, eh, Don?"

He shook Donald by the hand and nodded at the children, "I'll pop by later if there's anything else I think of."

The door closed and Donald's shoulders sagged. "That's the problem. Unless there were witnesses, we're stuck."

"It's so unfair. I just don't understand for vot reason people do this thing." Marie sighed.

"Old customs die hard. I'll tell you a secret. When I was young, we... I had a hobby, like most boys round here. I collected eggs, knew every nest site for miles around. We'd poke little holes in each end and blow out the yolk: display them in a case. Nobody told us it was wrong." He looked at Jan and Marie. "Different times. I grew up, but others didn't. And now our beautiful bird has too many enemies, all human. Not just the egg thieves, but some gamekeepers too who think any bird of prey is vermin. The pigeon-fanciers are the worst of the lot – one of them will happily coat the wings of one of their pigeons with pesticide – Carborfuran usually. They'll let it go near a falcon site where it's bound to be caught. Once it's been eaten, the poison does its work. They claim that the peregrine takes their homing pigeons. Well, of course she does! She's a wild animal – but she was there before them. Anyway..." Donald took the empty cups out to the kitchen, "I'm blathering on again. I can tell you that the male and female have been seen at the quarry again. So, as Jim Cheever said, we have to keep hope on our side."

Jan and Marie sensed it was time to leave.

"Thank you much for tea!" said Marie.

Donald waved them out of the door. "It was a pleasure." From the smile on his face, they could see he meant it.

As they left the shadowy shut, Marie felt in her pocket. It was still there – a scrunched-up piece of foil. What would PC Cheever have said? You could hardly call it evidence.

A shocking sight

A shot rang out, loud enough to make Jan jump. His bike wobbled and he lost control, veering straight for the hedge. He closed his eyes and slammed on his brakes. The rubber pads screeched against the steel rims and he came to a shaky full stop within centimetres of a nasty-looking hawthorn bush. The way the sound echoed round the valleys, it could have come from anywhere, though it felt close.

He climbed off his bike and sat down on the verge to catch his breath. Common sense told him that he wasn't the intended victim, unless the Mafia had opened up premises in south Shropshire. The sound of shotguns was one he'd got used to since moving to England. But it wasn't the pheasant-shooting season, so what was going on?

Jan wheeled his bike slowly down the lane looking for a gap. He wasn't that far from the Poultry Palace and had just finished another mind-numbing shift. His back and arms ached. Who'd believe that eggs could be so heavy?

He reached a gate and stopped. He looked around

him, then carefully lifted his bike over and stowed it behind the hedge. It was none of his business but he was sure that whoever had fired the gun had nearly made him crash. Besides, he was curious.

Beyond the hedge grew a crop of rape-seed, already flowering yellow in the weak April sun. Jan hated the stuff. It made his eyes water. He hugged the edge of the field and worked his way round. Another gate led to pasture, filled with sheep. The lambs bleated merrily and bounced about, proving that their legs had inbuilt springs.

At the far end, a barbed-wire fence marched across the landscape like a scar. Kneeling down by the fence, doing something that Jan couldn't make out, was a man. He almost melted into the background, dressed as he was in cap, coat and wellies of various shades of green. It was Jan in his trainers and jeans who stood out.

The man stood up abruptly, obviously done with his work, and Jan had to dive behind a scrap of hedge. There were so many gaps that he could easily see through. In the crook of the man's arm lay something that was bent like a bow, glinting in the sunlight. Even at this distance Jan knew what it was. He was also on private land and within easy range. His heart beat faster.

The man turned towards him, scanning the field.

Jan hunched further down. Had he seen him? This was mad! His trainers were already covered in mud and he realised that the patch of bare earth under the hedge was also the local sheep toilet. He was kneeling in it!

He tried to keep still, convinced that every heartbeat was louder than a gunshot. As he crouched there, his mind slowly caught up. Of course, he recognised him now, had seen him before: it was Witherman!

This was even worse. What if he came this way? There was nowhere to run, nowhere to hide. Jan risked turning his head and very slowly peered through the branches. Witherman was now leaning against a fencepost, eating something with a shiny wrapper. Then he turned and bent to inspect the fence, before marching off in the opposite direction, uphill. Jan took some deep breaths. That had been far too close for comfort.

He waited until the retreating figure had disappeared into the distance before making a move. He climbed carefully over the gate but the ewes began bleating madly, alarmed by the intruder. The noise was the last thing Jan needed and he nearly turned tail. But no one came running to investigate.

He skirted around the sheep, who calmly resumed munching further off, and then he approached the fence. A black shape was swinging on the wire.

Jan stepped closer. It was a bird, shot dead. Its black feathers hung limply. It looked like a crow, but the biggest crow Jan had ever seen. It hung from a noose of tightly-tied baling twine. Jan was horrified and fascinated at the same time. One thing was certain: he'd seen enough.

***

"Aren't you hungry, Jan?"

Mrs Kleček frowned. Jan normally wolfed down his food, especially after a shift at the Poultry Palace. But now he pushed his potatoes round his plate and looked pale.

"Sorry, Mum. Nothing wrong with your cooking, I promise."

Jan didn't want to tell them, but he couldn't help it.

"I saw a dead bird on my way home today…"

Lady Beddoes sat back in her chair. "Oh, the wonders of the modern car! Not only does it take us from A to B, but in the process, any poor creature that gets in the way is eliminated – though surely it's no different in the Czech Republic?"

"No Lady B. I meant that…" Jan looked round the table, not wanting to put people off their food, "The bird wasn't in the road, it was on a fence, hanging by some string. And it was big, like a giant crow!"

There was a strange look in Lady B's eye. "Ah, yes. Old customs die hard. It may look barbaric but…" Jan and Marie waited for an explanation.

"Well you see, it explains where the original word 'scarecrow' came from. Some of the farmers still use it. It's called a Gamekeeper's Gibbet."

"Vot is *jibbit*?" The word sounded ugly to Marie.

"Sorry. I keep forgetting. In seven months, you're all starting to sound quite English. A gibbet is the same as a gallows: a place for hanging." She put a hand to her neck, rubbing it absently. Marie shivered. "And so some of the old boys, hard as stone they are, they shoot a crow and then hang it up. It's a sign: Keep Off My Crops or else."

"But does it work?" Jan asked, "It certainly scared me." Though in truth he wasn't sure if it was the bird or Witherman that was more unsettling.

"In a strange way it does, though there's something dark about it. It certainly worries the crows and frightens them off."

An uncomfortable silence fell.

"Come on, then, Jan," Mrs Kleček got up briskly. "If you're not going to eat that, you can help to clear."

***

That night, Jan couldn't sleep. Every time he closed his eyes he saw the bird like a dark stain, swinging round and round in the breeze. Finally, he threw back his duvet and crept down the moonlit corridors of Bagbury Hall to Marie's room, trying to avoid the noisiest floorboards. He knocked gently.

"Who is it?" a voice cried hesitantly.

"It's only me!"

Jan pushed open the door as quietly as he could. What was it with old houses? They seemed to be held together by creaks, groans and squeaks. The hinges rasped as if complaining.

"I thought..." Marie sat up in bed hugging her knees.

"Oh, come on, Marie. We're safe here…"

"That poor bird!" said Marie.

"Yeah, and I missed out the rest of the story. I didn't want to get into trouble." He told her about the gunshot, his journey through the fields and the sight that had greeted him.

"Witherman? Are you sure?"

"Sure, and I was dead lucky."

"When most people hear a shot, they run away."

Jan shrugged his shoulders. "That's me. I can see it on my gravestone: *Jan Kleček, killed by a Fatal Attack of Curiosity.*"

Marie was glad her brother was here with her. When they were young, they'd always shared a room and stayed awake whispering every night. She'd never admit it now, but she missed those times.

Jan sat in silence for a few seconds. A shaft of moonlight prised its way in through a curtain chink, drawing a straight line across the floor.

"Any more hassle from Cassie?"

"No, but I'm not looking forward to going back to school. I suppose I could always actually push her off the wall!"

"That's more like it. I tell you what, the look on Doug's face when you kicked him in the shins was something else!"

"Thank you." Marie bowed. " First stop Doug.

Next stop, international bodyguard to the rich and famous! Now, promise me you won't go off on any more hare-brained excursions!"

"Yes, Ma'am. Whatever you say, Ma'am!" Jan stood up to go back to bed. "I promise!"

But promises are made to be broken.

Hidden horrors

"Be a good lad, and go and buy us some more milk! I'm dying of thirst here!" Rick Hegley nodded towards the door. Jan wondered if this was how servants felt in the old days, at the beck and call of their master's whims. He traipsed out of the office and climbed wearily on his bike. Still, it beat lifting pallets. The stink wafting from the main shed was worse today. He almost gagged as he cycled past.

Twenty minutes later, Jan held a carton in his hand, and was about to open the door to the Portakabin office. It was a warm day and the windows were wide open. He could hear Hegley on the phone spinning his latest deal. He paused for a moment to draw breath and held the cool carton against his forehead. No point in going inside just yet. He might as well take advantage of a few moments' reprieve. The voice inside dropped to a low murmer so that Jan could barely catch the words. Odd, he thought, when Hegley's confident tones usually boomed across the yard as if the man had an amplifier wired up to his tongue. Jan craned his neck nearer the window directly next to his head and sank down on to the step.

"... They should be... yes... I do know what I'm doing." Then silence, as someone spoke on the other end. Jan looked nervously round the yard. The whole place was eerily quiet, as if people (and animals) had been banned from the premises.

"That's what I said." Hegley's voice dropped even lower. "Two thousand per egg... yes... and more if they hatch."

Jan was confused. Hegley dealt in thousands of eggs. How could one egg be worth thousands? It didn't make sense... he must have misheard. Sometimes he still found it difficult to follow a whole conversation.

Hegley's voice rose suddenly. "Safe? It's Heg the Egg you're dealing with, not some amateur!" He snarled, "Got them under lock and key. One very special key..." The call ended abruptly with the sound of a phone being slammed down on a table.

Jan didn't move. *Lock and key*. What was all that about? Unless... no! Surely not!

Jan stood up very slowly, thinking hard and trying to come to a decision. Finally, he turned, coughed loudly and reached for the door.

"Got your milk, Mr Hegley." He forced a smile.

"Good, good. Don't dither, boy. Get that kettle going. Looks like you've earned yourself a brew with all that cycling!"

But it wasn't the exercise that had made Jan break out into a sweat.

"Thanks, Mr Hegley."

"And then you can get on with some filing."

For the rest of the afternoon, Jan helped Hegley bring some order to his overflowing papers. He tried to scan each file without seeming too interested, but receipts for de-beaking machinery, feed and antibiotics were not what he was looking for.

***

Later, on their way home, Jan pulled his bike off the road and motioned Will to follow.

"Can't take the pace, eh?" said Will. "Some of us know what real work is! Not that cushy office stuff you landed this afternoon."

"Shut up, Will. This is important!" Jan looked around him, as if the hedgerow might start sprouting ears. "It's about Hegley…" Then he repeated everything he could remember of the phone call.

Will's eyes widened.

"You mean…"

"Yes. And there was I accusing Doug!"

"But it still could've been him that stole them to order, you know, for the big boss man."

"I didn't think about that. It's possible, I suppose. But listen, Hegley mentioned a key and I've a got a plan. Do you remember the first day we turned up there?" Jan explained his idea. Will listened, nodding from time to time.

"OK, then," Will agreed. "Nine o'clock tonight! Let's go for it! You tell your mum you're coming over to mine for a DVD and I'll do the same. Let's just hope they don't cross-check."

The two boys pedalled off and Jan thought back to what he'd promised Marie the night before. But there was no going back now.

***

It was nearly dark when Jan and Will met at the Five Turnings, a lonely crossroads. The first bats of the year swooped like shadows in the charcoal sky.

"Are you sure about this? Shouldn't we ring the police?"

"What evidence do we have – an overheard phone call? They'll say it's my bad English. The man *deals* in eggs, so obviously I misheard."

"Maybe you did." Will shuffled uneasily on his bike.

"If you thought that, why are you here with me now?"

"Good point, Sherlock!"

"Who?"

"Oh, never mind."

They hid their bikes in woods behind the farm and made their way through a huge field of spring barley down one of the tractor ruts. Beside the Poultry Palace they paused. The place was even quieter than usual. Far off, a dog barked. The dark deepened into silence.

"We must look for the key!" Jan whispered. He crept with Will towards the Portakabin and turned the door handle. It was locked.

"This is why you need me!" Will pulled a plastic ruler out of his rucksack and wiggled it under the nearby window frame. "Who said TV wasn't educational!" he hissed. With a bit more jiggling, he caught the catch and the window swung open. A minute later and they were both inside, flopping on to the floor and trying not to giggle.

Jan grabbed his pencil torch. Up until now, the most illegal thing he'd used it for was to read under the covers at night. They searched the drawers first and found a mess of empty cigarette packets, receipts and unused stationary. The bottom drawer revealed a half-empty vodka bottle.

"Poor guy – the chickens must be driving him to drink!"

Jan's thin beam of light played over the office – filing cabinets, kitchen area, desk. Nowhere obvious.

The boys felt under the drawers for anything that might have been sellotaped there. Nothing. They peered behind the radiator, peeled back the loose edge of the carpet and felt in the pockets of the jacket hanging on the back of the door.

Will pointed to the metal box of tea bags. "What about in there?"

Jan snorted, "Not a chance! Or I'd have stirred it into a cup of tea by now!"

Will flung himself into the swivel chair. "This is impossible. We're on a wild goose chase."

"What gooses?" Jan asked, still moving the torch around the room.

"*Geese,* Jan, *geese!* Like big, swimming chickens. What's that?"

The beam of Jan's torch had come to rest on the picture of chickens clucking round an idyllic farmyard. He was staring at it.

"Of course! Chickens! Will, you are genius!" Jan carefully lifted down the picture. Yes, there on the hook behind it was a key! He wanted to jump around shouting "Eureka". But instead, he quietly slid the key into his pocket.

They slipped back out of the window and hugged the shadows all the way round the yard until they reached the big shed with a little side door.

Jan was just putting the key to the lock when there

was a sudden sound behind them. A door on the other side of the yard crashed open and light spilled out. The boys froze. A worker stomped outside, pulling off his regulation hairnet and paper mask. He spat on to the concrete, rubbed his hands together and pulled something shiny from his pocket. "I've been waiting for this," he murmered.

"What do you think you're doing?" came another angry voice from behind the first man.

Jan stopped breathing. He frantically tried to think of an excuse why he and Will could possibly be there.

"Fag break! I'm entitled. So put a sock in it!" The man lifted a silver lighter to a cigarette. The tip hovered in the darkness like a glow-worm.

The second man snarled, "Five minutes. That's your lot, so hurry up!" Then he spun round and stalked back in, slamming the door.

Silence fell. Still the boys didn't move. They could hear the man's steady in-out breaths and see the rising smoke. At last, he took a few hasty drags, stamped out the glowing butt and heaved open the door. It clanged shut behind him, leaving the yard in darkness.

"That… was… close!" Will was gulping air. He slumped against the wall. "Come on, get on with it."

Jan didn't reply. He fumbled the key into the lock. His fingers felt like jelly but the key did its job. Swiftly they slipped in and pulled the door behind them.

"Remind me what we're doing here, would you?" Will looked pale in the grey light.

"Because we know that Hegley has the only key to this door, so it must lead somewhere he doesn't want other people to go. It's the obvious place." Jan peered ahead. "Which way now?" A dim light filtered through plastic strips that hung across a door frame at the end of the corridor. It cast just enough of a glow to show another door on their left. Will and Jan looked at each other and pointed to the closed door. Jan turned the handle. It was very stiff but it clicked open and the door eased inwards on to a smallish, square room. Inside, the boys saw lockers and pegs on two sides, with overalls, masks and boots hanging up.

"Oh!" Jan's face fell, "This is no good."

Will nodded, "We don't even know how many are on the late shift tonight, or what time they finish. Mind you," he unhooked an overall, "perhaps we should borrow some of this stuff and get suited up. What do you think?"

Jan agreed that being dressed the part would make them less conspicuous, though everything was far too big.

"Hurry up!" Jan urged, as they struggled into the suits, "What's that noise?"

From beyond the door on the opposite side of the room came a strange, continuous hum.

Shafts of light outlined the frame.

"I don't know, but we're not heading in that direction to find out! Come on. Back the way we came!" Will turned and led the way. "Phew! That stink is something else!" He was right. It was the same acrid smell that hung around the yard, only stronger.

They swung the door closed and moved quietly on down the corridor. "What is it you English say?" Jan whispered. "After you!" He stood aside as they reached the plastic strips.

"Thank you so much. Not!"

A short corridor led down, ending in a glass fire door. They peered through but couldn't see anyone around. Here goes!" Will grimaced.

It was the roar that hit them first. *Clucking* could not possibly describe it; unless it was a cluck amplified a thousand times until the sound resembled a huge, single, scratching scream.

The stench came next. Jan almost gagged. Breathing as lightly as he could, he forced himself to look. The shed stretched a couple of hundred metres. Far overhead, neon strip lights bathed the whole scene in stark, white light. They stood in a walkway that ran through the middle of the building. And on either side of the channel, stacked in racks, one above the other were cages. Everywhere they looked there were cages bursting with chickens.

These were not happy birds strutting round a farmyard looking for seeds and worms to peck at. Jan tried to imagine what it would be like spending his whole life inside a locked room the size of the downstairs toilet alongside several others.

So, this was how the factory worked. Underneath the racks, conveyer-belts trundled endlessly into the distance. These carried the eggs, which looked remarkably pristine and clean compared with the state of the hens. Will stepped over to one of the racks. A bird had got its head wrapped round the wire mesh as if its neck were no more than a piece of elastic. The other birds pecked at it as it tried feebly to escape. Will bent to gently untangle the exhausted creature.

"This is…"

"Bad," said Jan. "Very, very bad!" In some of the cages, they saw what looked like dead chickens trodden into the mesh floor. The lower racks were the worst, as chicken droppings fell into them from the cages above. No wonder Hegley kept the door locked.

"I feel sick," said Jan.

"But it's not why we're here. Come on, we've got a job to do!"

Jan felt hopeless. He wanted to run out and cycle home to the safety of Bagbury Hall. But Will was right. They'd come this far: he couldn't give up now.

They split up, walking up and down the central

walkway, searching. They were looking for somewhere warm. "Warm…" Jan mused. He looked down. The floor wasn't actually a floor at all, but more of the same mesh that made up the floors of the cages. At the end of the walkway a set of stairs led down.

He motioned to Will and they stood at the top, peering into the darkness.

A tight squeeze

They had no choice. There was nowhere else to go. Jan switched on his torch and down they went.

This was the source of the smell. The basement ran the length of the building and the mesh floor above served a purpose. Jan was glad of his boots as they squelched past piles of deepening manure. The torch beam revealed another world – a landscape of muck, piled in miniature mountains that reached above Jan and Will's heads in places.

Luckily, there was a path running directly underneath the walkway. It led between the compacted droppings. Far over on one side, Jan saw a hen which had somehow escaped, trapped in the oozing liquid. She flapped uselessly, trying to push off the flies. If he tried to reach her, he would risk being sucked in himself.

"No one in their right minds would want to come down here!" Will said.

They both held their masks tightly over their noses and Jan led the way.

However, as they drew close to the end of the

pathway, all they could see ahead was a concrete wall. Will stopped and sighed. "Dead end. I told you this was a wild goose chase! And I'm sweating like a pig in this heat. Come on. I've had enough."

"But that's the point. It's the warmest place, Will. And what were you saying before about having a job to do?"

Jan's torch beam swung round to each side, suddenly illuminating a pair of eyes staring back! His breath caught in his throat, but the rat turned tail and scurried off somewhere safe and dark. Just behind where the rat had gone was what looked like a pile of planks, camouflaged by a splatter of muck.

"Hang on a second." With the fumes and noise, Jan's eyes were playing tricks. The pile of planks suddenly made sense and took shape as a shed-like hut, complete with door, encrusted padlock and a tiny, high window. If you weren't looking for it, you'd never know it was there.

Will came up behind him. "OK. I take it back. Maybe we've struck lucky!"

Jan stepped closer and peered up towards the window, but it was too high. "Maybe… here, give me a hand". Will bent his knees to take the weight. Jan balanced and scrabbled against the window. "Can't see a thing! It's covered in … eurgh!" He spat on to the corner of his sleeve and rubbed hard. "Oh! *Sakra!*"

"What?" Will demanded, "What can you see?"

But all Jan said was, *"Ano! To jsou ty vajíčka."* This was not striking luck, but gold. Inside, the tiny space contained just a table and two heat lamps trained on to a plastic crate filled with straw – and resting gently in the straw, three almost round, rust-spotted, brown eggs!

"Oi!" grunted Will. "My legs are dying down here, and thanks to your boots, are now coated in…"

"Yes!" Jan jumped down. He explained to Will in a rush what lay inside. "We must get the eggs out. By the time we ring the police, it might be too late!"

But the padlock was thick as a fist and the window too small to crawl through.

Suddenly the boys froze. There were footsteps

above them, clattering across the mesh floor. Jan clicked off his torch. Had they been seen? The neon lights from the roof barely made their way down into this basement, so for now they were in shadow. The boots headed in the direction of the stairway. If they came any further, the boys would be trapped.

"There must be another way out," whispered Will.

"How?"

"They have to get rid of this stuff, right? Haven't you seen the tractors coming and going? There's no way they could shift this lot by hand…" Will pointed back they way they'd come, past the bottom of the stairs and beyond. They crept along, listening to the walkway trembling above their heads.

The footsteps paused at the top of the stairs.

Right at the other end of the basement, two enormous sliding doors barred their way. Would they be locked? The boys reached the doors and crouched down, straining their ears. The reverberating steps moved off again.

"I think he's gone!" mouthed Will. They stood together and pushed hard at the doors. Nothing happened. Will stood back and dropped his arms, "It's no use." He grabbed Jan's torch and shone it along the walls. "Maybe there's another little side door." Then he ran the beam across the floor. "Jan! We're so stupid!" He grasped a door handle again, but this time he put his shoulder into it and heaved it sideways.

"They're sliding doors!"

There was a creaking groan and the door shifted, opening into a corner of the complex Jan had never seen. Sure enough, across the yard stood a tractor with a scoop attached. Two more seconds and they'd be on their way.

"Bit late for you boys, isn't it?"

It was the same man they'd seen earlier, when he'd nipped outside for a cigarette. He pulled off his mask and they recognised burly Mr Whittaker. This was a man who could happily stack two or three pallets at a time and lift them as lightly as a feather, while Jan struggled with a single one. There would be no getting away from him.

"We…" Jan began.

"…Got the bum job. You know Hegley, eh?" Will broke in, making it up as he went along. "Tractor broke down, and guess what we'll be shovelling for the next few days!"

A grin broke over the round expanse of Whitaker's face. The story was as thin as a sheet of paper and even more flimsy, but he bought it. "Yeah, that's Heg the Egg for you. You poor kids!" He frowned for a second. "But why are you shovelling this stuff in the dark?"

It was a good question. Will hesitated. "Not due to start until tomorrow. After our shift, thought we'd have a look to see what we were letting ourselves in for. First thing in the morning, we resign!" Will crossed his fingers.

"Well…" Mr Whittaker's frown didn't hang about for long. "Glad I'm not in your shoes! Gotta get back to work, eh?" He ambled away, leaving the boys to punch the air.

***

Marie woke to find an intruder standing by the bed. She opened her mouth to scream.

"Shhhh! It's only me!" whispered Jan. He was in his outdoor clothes.

She reached for the light and blearily looked at the alarm on the bedside table. 4.30 a.m. "Are you mad?"

"Not the last time I looked in the mirror!" Jan threw her a pile of clothes. "Get changed. I'll explain on the way!"

Marie turned over and closed her eyes. "Leave me alone!" she muttered.

"It's the peregrine eggs, stupid!" Jan said. "Will and I found them, but Will had to go home. He's leaving for a family trip to his Grandad's first thing this morning. And anyway, only you can help. I've got a plan."

Instantly Marie was awake. Five minutes later, they crept out of the house. It was still dark. Marie shivered as they pedalled off. "Are you sure about this?"

"Just wait and see!" As Jan described the evening's adventures, her eyes widened.

"So that's why I need you! Is that OK?" he asked.

"Of course!" But Marie wasn't as certain as she sounded.

Jan was breathing hard. He was exhausted. He had spent most of the night wide awake in bed, wondering what to do. Will had said they should phone the police but Jan was afraid there would be nothing for them to find by the time they actually got there. So instead, Jan had agreed to ring Will at 8.00 a.m. to make a final decision. This seemed the only way.

After hiding their bikes, they crept through the pre-dawn mist towards the farm complex. It was lucky for them that the main exit from the shed was hidden from the courtyard. They should be in and out in minutes, well before the 6 a.m. shift began.

As they approached the double doors, all was quiet. "Hold your nose!" Jan warned, and heaved his shoulder into one of the handles. As a gap appeared in the darkness, Marie wished she was still safely in bed. But then she thought of Donald. She couldn't let him down.

Jan closed the door behind them and switched on his torch. Although he'd told her what was there, it was no preparation for what greeted her. There was no time to think about it though, as she ran to keep up with Jan.

"This is it!" He stood, training his torch on the little wooden shed. "And there's the window. Think you can make it?"

"If there was an Olympic prize for wriggling, I'd win it easily!" Marie snorted. "Kneel down, *Janíčku*, and bow to my superior skills!"

Jan did as he was told and Marie clambered up on to his back. The window had a broken catch, so it swung in easily enough, but that left the tiny window-frame. Marie pushed her head through and scrunched her shoulders together. "Stand up higher!" She hissed, "I can't quite reach."

It was much more than a tight fit. The frame scraped and snagged as she tried squeezing her ribs through like a tube of toothpaste. Perhaps even she wasn't small enough. Panic rose at the thought of being trapped in this subterranean darkness. *Breathe slowly,* she told herself. *Breathe in!* Then suddenly, she was through, dropping head-first to the floor, breaking her fall with a forward roll that her gym

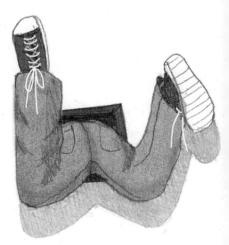

teacher back in the Czech republic would have been proud of. She came to rest against the legs of a table and picked herself up.

And there they were: the peregrine's eggs, not lying where they belonged in a scrape on a cliff, but stuck here in an evil little basement among the valleys of bird droppings.

"Come on!" hissed Jan. Marie looked around, deciding what to do. She moved to the other side of the table and eased it as gently as she could until it stood directly under the window. The eggs lay safely in the plastic crate. She clambered up on to the tabletop and carefully lifted out the first egg. She cupped the warm shell in her hand and leaned through the window. Jan reached up to receive it and placed it gingerly in an egg box he had pulled from his rucksack. Marie crouched down to lift the second egg. It was already in her hand when she heard a muffled voice.

"Good morning, Jan. Bit early for you to be about, isn't it?"

Jan swung round. Someone was standing halfway along the pathway, shining a torch right in his face. The torch beam moved closer and dropped to the egg box.

"Now, I wonder what you've got in there?"

It was Hegley.

Jan nearly dropped the egg carton but then, in a moment of instinct, he put it behind his back. How long had Hegley been down here? With the noise from above, it was impossible to tell, but Jan knew he had to distract him, get him away from the shed.

"I – I don't know what you mean."

"Well now, a little birdy had a word in my ear. Actually, Whittaker's not so little!" Hegley mused. "Somewhat slow maybe, but he's good at the grunt work, I'll give him that. He was on the way out from his night shift. Kept joking about how I was exploiting the youngsters by asking them to shovel you-know-what by hand. It took a while to put two and two together. But look what I came up with."

Hegley held out his hand. His fake smile had vanished and Jan saw that he meant business.

Jan had to act, and act now. He pulled the egg box out from behind his back and ran straight at Hegley, holding the box in front of him like a battering ram.

"Whoa... stop. That's precious, that is!" Hegley made the fatal mistake of stepping back, forgetting that only one thing lay behind him. He fell with a sickening squelch. "I'll get you, you little...!" But Jan was already powering past him down the passageway and out through the double doors.

All this time, Marie was leaning inside the shed, keeping as still as possible.

Hegley swore as he tried to extricate himself, finally rolling out of the muck and on to the walkway.

He shook himself like a dog and took off after Jan.

The yard was too quiet. Where were witnesses when you needed them? Jan hared off round the edge of the building. He had to draw Hegley as far as possible so that Marie could get away. He paused just long enough for Hegley to spot him and also to see how well and truly re-decorated the man looked. Jan would have smiled if he'd had time.

He ran round the back of the Portakabin and paused to catch his breath. He didn't think he'd make it through the fields. Where was the last place Hegley would look?

Something came back to him that his dad had always said: *It's darkest right under the candle flame.*

Of course…

The window was still unlatched. Jan clambered through. He hoped Hegley hadn't heard. He was exhausted. He crept under the desk and placed the egg box gently on the floor, before curling up right in the corner.

Escape but no escape

The tiny shed was quiet, apart from the muffled clucks of ten thousand hens far above. Marie looked at the remaining two eggs. Jan had the only box. If she tried to carry them in her pockets, they'd break, which was just what her heart felt like doing right now.

"Sorry, little ones! I promise we'll be back!" She climbed up and put her arms through the window, and found it easier to wriggle through this time.

The waste pits were deserted as she ran for the double doors. Should she wait for Jan or go to get help? What would he want her to do? Her mother had said she could have a mobile phone when she was eleven. Three more months. If only she'd nagged more...

She crept back through the field to the bikes and decided to wait. Jan could outrun Hegley easily, couldn't he? With that one egg, they'd have evidence. But Jan didn't appear and soon it was past 6 a.m. The sun winked above the hedges and a low mist lay like a patched blanket over the fields. Marie shivered in the early-morning breeze.

Jan only drifted off for a moment. He dreamed he was being chased by a giant chicken that was pecking at his feet… "No! No! Get off!"

He jolted awake. There was no giant chicken: only a hairy hand with a gold ring grasping his leg. The other hand gripped something furry. Was it a rat?

Jan panicked. "OK. I'm coming out!"

Hegley let go. He was smiling grimly. Jan was dazed. Was it Hegley? He looked different: he was bald as an egg! Then Jan realised what the 'rat' really was.

"Got you, you little thief!" Hegley clumsily slapped his toupée back on, back to front.

Jan retreated against the wall. "YOU stole them! How could you?"

"Ha! As sure as eggs is eggs, there's money to be made. And as for how, that's none of your business! Now, hand over that box!"

Jan clutched the carton to his chest. Donald had said that the longest the adult left the scrape was about half an hour. Any longer, and the eggs were in danger from jackdaw theft or growing cold. He wondered if the baby inside this egg had a chance.

"I'm going to ring the police!"

Hegley smiled. "Here's the phone. Be my guest!" He took the phone from its cradle and held it out.

Jan hesitated, confused.

"I didn't get to be rich by being stupid. Those eggs now have your fingerprints all over them. I always wear gloves when I handle the little beauties." Hegley put the phone back down. "So the question is, who will the police believe: a teenage tearaway and a foreigner to boot, or a respectable businessman? Now, give me the box!" he snarled. "If you don't, I'll call the police myself!"

Jan was defeated. There was no way out. The only consolation was that Hegley clearly thought Jan was by himself.

"Oh, and don't breathe a word of this to anyone, boy. Remember those fingerprints! I could make life very unpleasant for your family. And finally, you're sacked! As is your mate Will. My daughter Cassie was right about you lot – always poking your nose in. Now, move it, so I can make sure that those little earners are still viable. They'd better be!"

Hegley held out his hand again. Reluctantly, Jan handed over the box and slunk out.

Outside, it was a bright new day and the morning shift workers were already chatting in the yard, their breaths making clouds in the cold air. Jan saw none of it. The dew drenched his trousers as he walked through the fields. But at least he'd given Marie enough time to get out. He felt guilty about involving her and wretched about telling her. Still, Hegley would have a shock when he opened the box to find only one egg. Jan wondered which way Hegley would run: straight after him, or off to the shed to check. Perhaps he'd better go faster.

He broke into a jog until he reached the fence.

"Jan! You made it! I knew you would!" Marie was overjoyed. "Quick, we must keep the egg warm."

"Don't have it!" he mumbled.

Marie saw he was empty-handed.

"Let's go home." Jan turned away from her and mounted his bike.

"But... what happened?"

"It's over. We lost, OK? There's nothing we can do."

As they cycled, Jan explained about the fingerprints.

"But that's terrible! Unfair!" Marie punched the handlebars.

"So? Who told you life was fair? Time to grow up, Marie..." Jan was silent for the rest of the journey.

While Marie crept in at the back of Bagbury Hall and up to her room, Jan pulled off his dirty boots and sank on to the stone step. He would have to face telling Will later too. What a mess...

He was stiff with cold by the time the sound of movement from the kitchen roused him. He stood up slowly and went in.

"You're back early!" said Mrs Kleček, trying to kiss his forehead.

Jan shied away. "Please mum… yes. Apparently they've got some older workers in who can shift more than us teenagers."

"That's disgraceful! Mr Hegley should be ashamed of himself!"

Jan nodded. It was too true.

"I hope he paid you for your work so far!"

Jan couldn't meet his mother's eyes. "Yes, yes…" He hated lying. That new Ipod seemed further away than ever.

Marie walked into the kitchen, yawning.

"How did you sleep, *Maruška?*"

"Fine, thanks." Marie darted a look at Jan.

"Breakfast! How about an omelette? At least you have these free eggs." But before Mrs Kleček could move, Jan snatched up the bowl of eggs from the kitchen table and hurled them out of the open window.

"You wouldn't want to know where those came from!" he shouted, and stormed upstairs, barging past his father in the doorway.

"What on earth was that all about?"

"Jan's lost his job. He's rather upset."

"Well, that sort of behaviour is just not on!" Mr Kleček said. "Shall I go and have a word?"

Marie answered. "Leave him, *Táto*. I'll go and talk

to him." She darted up the grand stairs in the central hall until she stood outside Jan's door. She knocked.

"Go away!" came the muffled reply.

"It's me!"

"I don't care…"

Marie twisted the handle and went in anyway. Jan was curled up on the bed. He wiped his face. "That rapeseed makes my eyes sting…"

"I believe you." Marie sat down on the bed.

Jan sniffed. "How can he get away with it? It makes me so…"

"Angry! Me too. PC Cheever helped us before. Surely he'd believe us?"

"I don't know. The eggs will be long gone by now. Where's our proof? It all sounds so far-fetched."

"It wasn't! We found them! That's the truth." Marie grabbed her brother's hand. "You've got to say sorry. Mum and Dad are really upset."

Jan nodded. All he wanted to do was sleep.

"And after that, it's time we went for help!" Marie had her determined look and Jan knew he was defeated all over again.

***

"I've always had a bad feeling about that man!" Donald sighed as he sat back in his armchair. "You two are both brave warriors! They could have done with you at Stokey Castle in the old days!"

Jan tried to smile. The tea was warm, and Donald assured them that the scones, spread with last autumn's blackberry jam, had been made with free-range eggs.

"But ve are back to, how you say, square vone!" Marie clenched her fist, as if she would punch anyone who disagreed.

"No, you're not!" Donald thundered. "We now know who did it! But he's wriggled out of it for the moment. Those damn fingerprints... Did both of you handle the eggs?"

Jan and Marie nodded.

"Thing is, I can't see him climbing up a cliff face in that smart suit of his, can you?"

"You mean..." said Jan, "...he didn't do it alone?"

"Possibly. But I'm an old man trying to protect a vulnerable bird. What do I know?"

Jan thought again. Could Doug have been lying when they confronted him outside the supermarket? His head spun with possibilities.

Donald continued, "When Hegley said he could make trouble for you, I wouldn't doubt it for a second. That man is a powerful force round here. And of course, he'll have moved the eggs by now."

"We found them the first time. Maybe we could do it again," Jan suggested, without conviction.

Donald stared at a photograph on the wall. It was of a peregrine nesting on a tiny ledge halfway up a cliff. The eggs were safely hidden under her body. She looked out at the camera with her sharp eyes, defying anyone to come near.

"Maybe…" A hush fell over the room. Donald was miles away. "Trust in your dreams… trust in your dreams!" he seemed to mutter to the picture. Then, "Ah!" He shook himself… "Where were we?"

Jan winced as he remembered the giant chicken which had turned into Hegley. That sort of dream, he could do without. "It was terrible inside the shed."

Donald shook his stick. "Terrible, yes. Illegal, no. He, and other intensive poultry farmers across this country ought to be ashamed of themselves.

109

Whether it's battery or so-called 'barn eggs', the result is the same – torture for the poor creatures. If they put pictures on the egg boxes to show where the eggs really come from, sales would drop through the floor." Donald paused. "But it's not a fight we can win. I wish I could be of more help. This arthritis has put years on me."

The children both suddenly understood that Donald's stick wasn't a countryman's accessory but a support that he couldn't do without.

"You let me know, eh? If there's anything I can do… " Donald stood up, and his head nearly touched the ceiling.

"How do you fit in here?" Marie asked.

Donald glanced at the low beams. "Surprising what you get used to. It may be small, but it's mine. As they say, *an Englishman's home is his castle!* And this is a rather scaled down version!"

Jan tried to swallow a yawn.

"It's time you two went home and got some sleep!" And he turned and shepherded them out of the door.

Not such a Good Friday

They stood tall as two towers on either side of the valley. Marie had never seen people so huge – noses big as houses, legs like tree-trunks. Their mouths opened and closed, but whatever shouts lay inside were silent. Marie paddled her toes at the edge of the lake. She looked up again as the giants dissolved into billowing cloud. The wind pushed and twisted the cloud like plasticine to re-form it into a falcon, large enough to blot out the sun. The bird came to life, its call echoing round the woods. For a second it fixed Marie with its stare. Then it leapt into the sky and hovered, before pulling its wings in for a long dive. Just as it vanished beneath the surface of the lake, Marie noticed the tiny golden key clamped in its beak...

Marie woke up. Her head was muzzy. Snatches of the dream came back to her. Of course... She quickly pulled on her clothes and ran down the corridor to Jan's room. Without bothering to knock, she pushed open the door and leapt on to his bed.

"Whatisit?" the figure buried under blankets groaned.

"Serves you right for waking me up so early yesterday!"

A tousled head with bleary eyes popped out. "I hate little sisters…"

"And good morning to you too! Listen, I had a dream!"

"You want a prize or something?"

"Don't be silly. Donald said *to trust your dreams*. He was right. When we went to Stokey Castle, he told us a story all about the giant bird that guards the treasure…"

"I'm too old for storytime…" Jan pulled the covers back over his head.

"Listen!" Marie grabbed the duvet and tugged it off the bed. "I think I know where he'll have taken the eggs!" Jan carried on grumbling as he hugged his knees to keep warm, but what Marie told him made sense.

"*An Englishman's home is his castle.* That's what Donald said! And that's where the treasure will be: at Hegley's home."

Jan was wide awake now. "Good thinking – I mean, dreaming. But where does he live?"

"That's what we need to find out!"

***

"Don't worry, I won't offer you eggs this morning!"

Mr Kleček put the kettle on to boil as Jan and Marie came into the kitchen. "But we've got some nice local bacon."

"Sorry about yesterday, Dad…" Jan thought about trying to explain, but it was all so complicated and there was Hegley's threat to explain, too.

"Apology accepted. Did Mum pass the message on from your schoolfriend Doug?"

"Friend? Doug? He rang… here! What about?"

"Wanted you to ring him. Left a number." Mr Kleček laid the rashers in the pan while Jan got on with cutting a loaf for toast. Jan and Marie exchanged looks.

"By the way, what's this brick doing in the oven?" Mr Kleček pulled out a house-brick with his oven gloves.

"*Táto*, please. You're interfering with my holiday homework. I have to see how long the brick stays warm!"

Mr Kleček shook his head, smiled at Marie and put the brick back in the Aga. So his daughter was turning into a scientist!

After breakfast, Jan picked up the phone in the hall and punched in the number.

"Is that Doug?"

"Who else would it be?" the gruff voice answered.

"This is Jan…"

"Yeah. The accent gives you away, mate."

"Why did you call?"

"I was thinkin' about our little chat. You asked me if I saw anything at the quarry. Well, it so happens that I did. The reward, you know?"

"How do we know it wasn't you, all along?"

"Then I wouldn't be ringing you, right? Work it out…" Then Doug told the story of what he'd seen and Jan suddenly realised that this was the missing piece of the jigsaw. Even the foil that Marie had picked up made sense now.

"OK. I believe you. I don't know why, but I do. Actually, we need to go somewhere to Hegley's house to look for something. Do you know where it is?"

Doug not only knew, he insisted on showing them himself. A plan was agreed and Jan said goodbye.

"Well?" Marie stood with her hands on her hips. "What do you think?"

"Interesting. I don't know, but what he just told me rings true. And with Will away, we could do with someone else as back-up. We need to go right now! Have you got the brick?"

"Safely wrapped up in my backpack. Let's hope it stays warm."

Before they left, Marie rang to leave a message on Donald's answerphone, to tell him where they were going and why.

***

There were no crenellations and the property wasn't surrounded by a moat, but Hegley's pad was impressive enough. Even the drive they were now creeping along was suitably lengthy and the spiked, iron fence that surrounded the estate must have cost him a fortune. As they drew nearer, letters on a three-metre-high gate spelled out THE ROYAL ROOST.

"How are we going to get over that?" Jan asked.

Doug gave a wicked smile. "I might not be good at much, but if there were exams for breaking and entering, I'd be top of the class!" Jan imagined that Doug was going to start on some complicated lock-picking exercise. But Doug went up to it, examined it, stepped back and gave it an almighty kick with his steel-toe-capped boot. The gate swung open. "Easy when you know how!"

Jan stayed out on the drive on lookout in case Hegley turned up unexpectedly. He ought to have been at the Poultry Palace for the next two hours. But if the worst came to the worst, he would jump out and act as decoy.

As Marie and Doug closed the gate behind them, Jan wormed his way into the rhododendron bushes lining the drive. He scrambled up a small bank overlooking the approach to the house and the surrounding farmland, took out his binoculars and waited nervously.

Marie wasn't impressed by the large, ugly, red-brick box in front of them that passed for Hegley's castle. It boasted fake, leaded windows and mock-Tudor beams. She felt uneasy with the huge figure of Doug striding along beside her. What if it was a trap? But Doug didn't notice Marie's suspicious glances.

"Come on then, girl. Your brother reckons you've

got a bit of the psychic gift, or whatever. Where we going to look?"

She could tell he wasn't taking her seriously. But the dream had been so vivid. "Ve must walk round. Maybe if I see it, I vill know." There were no cars parked outside and the garage door was open. Marie edged along the lawn and peered inside the ground- floor window of the main house.

"Oh!" She motioned to Doug to get out of sight. Behind the curtains, a figure sat glued to a TV screen. Marie recognised the expensive jeans and the long brown hair. Cassie. The thought of that horrible girl made her shiver. The TV was on at full volume, but they had to be careful. Still, the good thing about Cassie being at home was that the eggs were unlikely to be in the house itself. Cassie was far too nosy. There were only a few sparse trees to the front of the property and she doubted Hegley would keep the eggs in the garage.

"This place is too big. It's hopeless!" muttered Doug. "We might as well give it up."

Marie stared at him. "Ve're not stopping now!"

As they edged round the wall, Marie noticed a path leading to the back of the house. Beyond were vegetable gardens and a tall leylandii hedge with a gate in the middle. Marie was drawn to the gate. On the other side, surrounded by the hedge, lay a swimming-pool. With the sun beating down, it looked inviting.

"Fancy a swim?" Doug joked.

Marie wasn't listening. She was remembering her dream: the two giants with the lake between; the huge bird and the key disappearing down into a pool... a pool! And here was one right at her feet... She ran round the edge, looking for anything that might jolt another clue into place. This swimming pool had been excavated. But at the far end, the ground fell away in a sharp slope. She jumped down to where a space had been cut into the slope. There was a door and behind it, the hum of machinery: filtration, equipment for heating. And if the pool was heated...

"A perfect place to keep eggs warm! Doug! Over here."

He jumped down next to her and studied the lock. The door was solid steel and opened outwards. "This needs more than a good kicking, I tell you. We need a key, and if Hegley keeps the key on him, then we're out of luck."

"But vot if he keeps one hidden nearby? He did at the egg place. Jan found it."

OK, Miss Marple! Worth a try."

They began searching. The hedge proved to be little better than a blank, green wall with no obvious hiding-place. Marie ran her hand under the three stone benches that stood along one side. Nothing.

Doug scratched his ear, "What about a loose

paving slab? You…"

He was interrupted by a loud shriek nearby.

"Quick, hide!" Marie whirled round and tugged Doug's arm, but he stood his ground and pointed.

"That wasn't human. Look!" A short way beyond the hedge, a copper beech tree spread its dense branches over the garden. And there, perched right on the top staring at them, was a bird: a peregrine! "What do you reckon? Think she's on our side?"

Marie simply nodded, too much in awe to say anything, while the impenetrable black eyes studied them.

The tree had given Doug an idea. "It's the only other thing nearby. I'm gonna check it out. My Grandad used to hide a spare key on a nail halfway up his apple tree. Maybe Heg's done the same..." Doug vanished. He was soon lost in the branches that bent low, almost to the ground. Leaves shook and the peregrine squawked and flapped in annoyance at the intruder, before taking flight over the pool. She dipped down towards Marie for a moment, almost close enough to touch. Then she soared up and disappeared into the distance.

Why would the bird come here? Marie wondered. Were her eggs hidden here?

Marie walked slowly round the lip of the pool. At the sloping end, the stone edging lifted slightly above the grass. There was a thin gap where the turf had shrunk away from the warm stone. She knelt and pushed her fingers into the gap. It was just wide enough to hide a key. She crawled along the edge, running her fingertips along until she felt something small and metallic. She scrabbled to pull it out and lifted it into the light. "*Sakra!*"

But it was just an aluminium ring-pull from a drinks can. Marie threw it angrily into the water and watched it float for a moment towards the filter hole at the edge. It bobbed on the lapping water and was sucked into the filter before it had time to sink.

Staring at the ripples brought back her dream again and the image of the bird diving into the water *with a key*. Marie leaned forwards and dipped her hand into the pool. She could feel the slight pull of the water into the filter. What if…?

She lay down at the edge to reach in and push up the plastic flap. It was awkward feeling around and she didn't want to fall in. But what was that? She dislodged a small, plastic box that was wedged there. She fished it out and opened the lid. Yes! Not treasure, but the next best thing: a key.

***

Jan looked at his watch. Twenty minutes had passed since Doug and Marie had gone. He hoped they were OK. He peered through his binoculars. The drive was clear. He scanned further round. A glint caught his eye at the far edge of the fields and he adjusted the focus. It was something shiny and it was in the hands of the very last person Jan wanted to see.

The man finished eating, scrunched up the foil wrapper and threw it to the ground. He began striding straight towards The Royal Roost, stick in hand. If he got too close, he'd see… This was bad news! Jan had no choice but to head him off. He pulled his hood up in an attempt at disguise, jumped to his feet and began waving and hooting as loudly as possible. Even from this distance, he could see the figure pause in its stride. That's it! thought Jan. Over here! Here I am, on private land! The next moment, the figure changed direction and broke into a run, heading straight for him. Jan set off, moving deliberately away from the house. He had to give Doug and Marie a chance.

However, the man had far longer legs than Jan and was soon gaining steadily. Jan made it to the end of the drive and ran, head down, along the lane, narrowly missing a car that furiously honked its horn. He hesitated for a moment in panic then dived into bushes on the far side. His pursuer was nearly at the edge of the field but, unless he planned on coming straight through the hedge, he'd have to veer round to the gate. This would give Jan time to lengthen the distance between them. He pushed on through and ran across a boggy field, scattering sheep. Ahead lay a small copse of trees. He glanced behind him. No sign yet. Good. Jan wanted to lead him as far away as possible. But first he'd need to catch his breath. He crashed on through to the other side of the trees and sank down against a trunk. His heart was hammering. He needed to press on but his legs felt as if they were melting.

"I've been hunting game all my life!" a low voice

said from behind him. "Think I'd have trouble finding a noisy piece of vermin like you?"

It was Witherman, smiling triumphantly. He stepped closer.

"Come on. You can't hide in the trees for ever."

Jan looked up into the deep-lined face and took a chance, "You like your cream eggs, don't you?"

Witherman's smile vanished. "What's that got to do with anything?"

"It's quite easy to get fingerprints from foil – the foil that we found at the quarry…"

"So? I like to eat chocolate eggs and I went to a quarry. Doesn't prove much, does it!"

With a lurch, Jan realised several things simultaneously. No one knew where he was. Witherman was twice his size. The odds were bad. And as Witherman reached out his huge, weathered hands to grab the boy, Jan remembered the car that had nearly run him over. It was Hegley's.

Meanwhile...

The key wasn't gold as in her dream, but pale silver. Marie hoped it would fit. She slipped down to the door and pushed it into the lock. It gave a satisfying *click* and the metal door swung out. She ducked in, waiting for her eyes to adjust to the light. Yes! There among the heating pipes, in a bed of straw, lay the treasure she'd dreamt about. There was no time to lose. She shrugged off her backpack and pulled out an empty egg box. Carefully, she placed each of the three eggs inside and then folded the box in the warm towel from the backpack. The wrapped brick at the bottom acted as a mini incubator. It should keep the eggs warm until they got home.

She closed the door and lifted her rucksack. The gate squeaked and she turned excitedly to tell Doug that she'd done it all by herself.

"What are *you* doing here, Svot-face?" Cassie was standing by the pool. "I don't see no older brother to protect you now. And why are you nosing round *my* pool? Jealous, are we?"

Marie backed away. "I…"

"You what?" Cassie stalked round the edge towards her. There was only one way out. But Cassie was between her and the gate. Marie turned and darted the other way around the pool. Cassie wasn't known for her quick-wittedness. She followed, leaving the way clear for Marie to reach the gate. Marie rushed through and pushed it shut behind her, giving herself an extra second while Cassie wrestled with the latch. Where was Doug? Surely he must have seen her?

Marie ran through the vegetable gardens between raised beds of rhubarb. Her pack was strapped on tightly and the eggs well insulated but if she fell, the box would be crushed. However, it seemed to be true that too much TV was unhealthy: Cassie was struggling to catch up. Marie found a gap in the hedge behind a garden shed and squeezed through. If she could make it past the house and to the gate, she'd be fine. Doug could look after himself.

She retraced the path round the side of the house and ran through the gravelled courtyard. Twenty minutes earlier, it had been empty. Now, a giant 4x4 car stood outside the garage. Its door was wide open.

Why hadn't Jan warned them? Or maybe he had. She remembered hearing some hooting noises earlier. But it was too late to worry about that now. It wasn't far to the entrance, only round the corner, and Cassie was still panting and puffing far behind. She could do it.

The eggs would be saved, and as for Hegley...

Kicking in the gate had not been Doug's brightest idea and his mistake was about to cost them dear. Marie skidded to a halt. Right in front of her, examining the broken lock, was the boss of the Poultry Palace himself. He looked up, saw Marie with her backpack and squared his shoulders to block the only exit. She swivelled round. Maybe there was a gap in the fence somewhere else. But behind, Cassie was suddenly bearing down on her. She was trapped.

"This is the girl I told you about, Dad! I caught her trespassing by the pool!"

"Really! The scummy Czech kid? Hmm. More than trespassing, I think. What's in the bag?"

Marie was desperate. She looked at Cassie. "I bet you didn't know it was your father who stole the peregrine eggs!"

"Clever Daddy!" Cassie pouted. "I do know he promised me a safari holiday if his latest deal made pots of money. He wants to have a go at shooting really big animals!"

"You're disgusting!" Marie shouted, close to tears. Behind Cassie, a movement in the trees caught her eye. She was momentarily hopeful. Could it be Doug? But the rustling in the leaves only produced a blackbird which landed on the lawn to hunt for worms. She was on her own.

"And you're on private property!" Hegley announced. "Once I retrieve what's rightfully mine, there'll be no evidence apart from a bunch of fanciful stories. I've told your brother to keep his mouth shut. When I put the word out round here, your whole family will wish they were back where they came from. And hopefully, that's where you'll be by the time I've finished! Now, hand it over!"

He waited while Marie reluctantly pulled off her backpack. So close and yet so very far… It wasn't fair.

As she bent down to loosen the drawstring, a sudden sound of sirens pierced the air. Everyone froze. Seconds later, Hegley's expression turned to panic as a police van zoomed into view.

"Keep your stupid mouth shut!" Hegley hissed at his daughter. "Let me do the talking."

The car screeched to a halt. Hegley shook himself and quickly assumed a look of relief. He pulled open the gate and motioned to the driver to wind down the window. It was PC Cheever.

"Thank God you're here, Jim – I've just caught the peregrine egg thief!"

Jim pushed the door open as Hegley politely backed away. "Well, the call I received did give me some interesting information, Rick." PC Cheever glanced around, noting Cassie glowering over Marie, who was fiercely clutching her backpack.

"He lies!" Marie said. "I found the eggs by his pool!"

Hegley laughed a man-of-the-world laugh. "It's a good story, Jim, but I've been suspicious of this family ever since the boy came to work on my farm. In fact, I think they even used my premises to keep the eggs warm. Cunning, eh?"

Before PC Cheever could answer, Hegley ploughed on, "And now, look who has the eggs, covered in their fingerprints! The evidence is all there, if you care to open the bag." By this time, Hegley had his arm round the policeman's shoulder as though they were old friends.

"Well now, Rick, I must say, this is extraordinary…" said PC Cheever.

"You can't believe *him!* You can't…" pleaded Marie.

"Everything my Dad says is true!" cried Cassie.

"Heg's lying!" a low, quiet voice broke in.

Four sets of eyes turned and looked up as tree branches shook, and Doug jumped down from his leafy hiding-place behind them. Talking to the police was his least favourite occupation in the world, and he looked startled at having opened his mouth.

"And you'd believe the word of this local vandal against that of an upstanding pillar of the community?" Hegley's look of outrage was remarkably convincing.

PC Cheever looked slowly from one to the other. Then Doug held something out towards them.

"Incredible what these things can do. I mean, I called the police, didn't I?" Doug still seemed amazed, as if his own do-goodery was a shock to his system. "But they also do a mean bit of videoing when you need 'em!" He pressed some buttons on his mobile as he walked up to Jim and turned the screen round for all to see. The five minutes before the arrival of the police car were played out in miniature. The voices were very faint, but the words were clear enough.

PC Cheever smiled. "As to whether cramming ten thousand chickens in cages makes you a pillar of the community, I wouldn't like to say. Lying and theft, however, are another matter. Your daughter's too young to charge, but you, sir, are not. We've got our very own cage for people like you, Mr Hegley. It's called – a cell!"

Cassie turned in fury toward Marie. "It's all your fault, you stupid little foreigner," she squawked. "Ever since you started at school here, you've been a pain…"

Marie took a deep breath. She had been tormented in the playground, trapped in a stinking shed and chased until her legs were ready to drop off. Enough was definitely enough. In one swift movement, she handed the rucksack to Doug and raised her other hand, bringing it across her tormenter's face with a slap that resounded round the yard.

Cassie burst into tears. "You saw that! Mr Policeman, this little scumbag just assaulted me! Arrest her."

Jim Cheever looked across at Doug. "I didn't see anything. Did you?"

"Not me, officer."

"How dare you!" Hegley tried to interrupt, but Jim Cheever stared him down. "I believe it's called *a taste of one's own medicine.* Now, do I need to call Social Services for her?"

Hegley was beaten and he knew it. "No, no. Give me two minutes to ring my ex-wife to come and pick her up." He turned and walked heavily towards the house.

***

Several minutes earlier, half a kilometre away, Jan had been pulled roughly to his feet by Witherman, who was now dragging him back towards the Royal Roost.

"My boss'll have something to say about your little spying exercise. Once we're there, we'll all have a chat and decide what to do with a mouthy boy who throws accusations around."

Jan's shoulders hurt where the man's hand gripped like pincers. But he had no choice. He wished it was like the movies, where one good karate chop would fell the bad guy. Maybe he could aim a sharp kick and twist free. Witherman, however, took no chances and the speed with which Jan was pulled over the ground was too fast for him to try anything.

At last they came to a small gate in the fence at the back of the vegetable patch. "Don't try anything smart while I unlock this, eh?" Witherman opened the gate and pushed Jan through the gardens and round the side of the house. Ahead of them, Witherman spotted Hegley making for the door.

"Mr Hegley!" he called, "Look what I've caught snooping round! This boy knows too much. What do you want to do with him this time?"

Jan wondered why Hegley was making funny motions with his hands.

Hegley flushed bright red and clamped a finger to his lips. But it was too late. As Witherman dragged Jan round the corner, he suddenly understood Hegley's frantic sign language.

"*This boy knows too much,*" Jim Cheever repeated. "That *is* interesting, Mr Witherman. Why don't you explain exactly what he does know?"

The whole company turned towards Witherman, who dropped his hand from Jan's shoulder and stepped back. His flinty eyes scanned the scene.

"Nothing. Nothing at all. This boy was just trespassing and I…"

"Stole the eggs!" said Jan.

Witherman sneered. "No proof. What's a couple of bits of foil? Pathetic. Need more than that."

Doug squared up to the huge man. "I'll give you proof. Me and a couple of mates quad-biked at the quarry the other weekend. Guess what?" Doug smiled. "It was only when Jan asked me that I worked it out. I saw you – halfway up a cliff! I'm the evidence…"

"Careful, Doug!" warned Jim Cheever, "You're in danger of losing your nickname!"

Doug didn't take his eyes off Witherman. "No, PC Cheever. There's thugs and then there's outright scummy villains!" he spat out.

Witherman's face hardened. "Well you don't scare me. None of you." He took a step forwards and suddenly seemed to tower over all of them. He gripped his stick and Marie again saw the sharp beak of the carved head. He advanced slowly, swinging the end of the stick from side to side.

"Now, Mr Witherman, you don't want to do something you'll regret," said PC Cheever, and he fumbled for his radio, requesting back-up.

Although Witherman was outnumbered, something in his eyes froze everyone to the spot. Even Doug stood there like a puppet.

"Vermin, all of you. No better than rats, and it's my job to keep this place clean." Marie noticed a fleck of spittle hanging from the side of his mouth. He raised the stick above his head.

The two giants meet again

Witherman looked over their heads. "Oh my! PC Cheever's sent in the troops."

Everyone turned round. In the drive stood another man. He was the same height as Witherman, though slightly stooped, and the stick he carried was an exact mirror of Witherman's.

"I thought I told you to stay in the back of the van!" PC Cheever began.

"Always the coward, weren't you... Donald?" sneered Witherman.

"If you call sticking up for defenceless creatures an act of cowardice, then I plead guilty. And threatening children is hardly the bravest thing you've ever done. You always were a bully. " Donald stared Witherman in the eye. "Put the stick down, Dirk."

"Or you'll what? Fall over?" Witherman advanced closer to the others. There was a sound of distant sirens from the direction of Priestcastle but they wouldn't arrive for some time. Surely, Jan thought, if they all rushed Witherman, he wouldn't stand a chance...

but nothing moved except the swaying beak on the end of the stick, ready to swoop on its prey…

Suddenly Marie thought she was dreaming. Was that a key flying through the air above her head? One moment Witherman was hovering above them, poised to strike, the next, he was lying flat out on the ground with two sticks instead of one and a big red mark on his forehead.

There was a moment's silence as everyone took in what had happened. Donald still stood behind them, his right arm trembling.

Doug was the first to speak. "Good shot, mate! Wow! Really good shot."

Donald smiled. "I lost every race at school – but javelin was another thing altogether. I got the county medal."

As a second police van pulled up and uniforms piled out, PC Cheever moved over to shake Donald by the hand. "Well done, Mr Witherman."

"Mr *Witherman?*" said Marie. "But that's him lying on the ground!"

"Well, my younger brother was always good at *lying.*"

"Oh!" Marie gasped. "Your brother…"

Witherman groaned and rolled over in the gravel while one of the other officers read him his rights and produced a pair of handcuffs. "It was Hegley!" he moaned, as he came to. "He told me to do it." Hegley aimed a kick at the hunched Witherman, but the gamekeeper grabbed his ankles and brought him thudding down in return. They had to be pulled apart and marched off to separate cars to be taken to the police station, along with Cassie.

As Witherman was pushed into the back of the second van, he gripped the door and stared out at Donald. "I'll get you for this!" he spat at them.

Donald held his gaze. "You've been getting at me for years, Dirk. Now it's my turn. While you're locked up, think about how the falcons feel, having everything stolen from them!" As he spoke, he straightened his spine to his full height. He looked ten years younger and full of fire. It was Witherman who slumped.

Donald pointed to the bag. "You children did well. But we haven't come this far to let a clutch of rare eggs go cold. Come on. Perhaps PC Cheever will give us a lift."

Doug, Jan and Marie were bundled with the backpack into the back of the van. PC Jim Cheever turned on the blue light and they sped along the lanes on their mission of mercy.

***

The following day was Easter Sunday. Mrs Kleček was determined to celebrate in style, so the huge kitchen table was laden with food.

"This is a feast, Eva, a wonderful feast!" said Lady Beddoes. She looked round the room at the assembled crowd: the whole Kleček family, plus Donald and Will, who was most put out to have missed all the action.

"Honestly! It's *so* unfair. Why did I have to go away at the crucial moment? I helped find them the first time. I was only gone a day. You could have waited!"

Lady Beddoes smiled. "The important thing is that

the eggs have been saved. In spite of" – she looked hard at the children – "or perhaps because of the appalling risks you all took."

František Kleček shuddered. "We're all proud of you. But promise never to be so foolish again!"

Donald agreed, "They were very lucky. What's more, the eggs were lucky, too. I took them straight to the Bird of Prey Centre, with free transport from Jim. Amazingly, after all the upheaval, they're hanging on in there. Right now, the precious cargo is nestled under a heat lamp and they are expected to hatch quite soon."

"But vot vill happen to the babies? Can they be returned to the parents?" Marie wanted to know.

"Sadly no. It's been too long. The female and her tiercel would reject them... They'll be well looked after – hand-reared... I know it's not the same." Donald fell silent.

Mrs Kleček signalled to her husband. "Time to eat!" A huge shoulder of lamb arrived in style. Mr Kleček delved into the bottom of the oven and brought out the freshly-baked bread rolls.

"Oh, look!" Donald clapped his hands. "they're in the shape of birds!"

"Yes!" Mr Kleček said. "With cloves for eyes. It's our Easter custom – and very good timing as well!"

Mrs Kleček carved the lamb and spooned out portions of *hlavicka* – a mix of semolina, eggs, herbs and smoked pork. As the plates sat hot and steaming, Marie's mother said a short grace in Czech and then motioned to everyone to tuck in. "*Dobrou Chut!* Good eating!"

"You're still not forgiven for having all that fun without me!" Will complained, between mouthfuls.

"I thought our night-time visit was enough fun for a lifetime!" Jan frowned, remembering, and turned to Donald. "But I can't believe the egg factory can just carry on like that."

Donald sighed. "According to Jim, it's very likely that Hegley will get a custodial sentence. Let's hope so. However, I suppose he'll simply employ someone else to manage the place while he's *away*, so to speak."

"And that's OK, is it?" Jan felt his face grow hot.

"I didn't say that, and as you well know, that kind of misery for the sake of eggs a few pence cheaper fills me with disgust."

"Yes. Well, I'm going to tell all my mates at school to stop buying anything but free-range!"

"That's my son!" Mr Kleček said, leaning over to pat him on the back.

Lady Beddoes coughed. "Perhaps this is a good moment to tell you all about a little plan of mine." Everyone turned to look at her as she continued.

"You won't know this, of course, because our man Hegley has kept it very quiet, but a little bird told me that he's been trying to sell the Poultry Palace. I imagine that he'll be even more keen now!"

"So?" Jan butted in. "How does that change anything?"

"Patience, Jan! I plan to buy it!"

All the faces around the table stared. "You?" said Donald, "But why?"

"Oh, that's easy," smiled Lady Beddoes, "I intend to turn it into a free-range poultry business: proper outdoor hutches in that huge field at the back and lots of trees planted to provide a habitat for scratching and foraging. Of course, I'll have to start by giving away half the chickens: there are just too many of them. I shall advertise: free hens to good homes. You'll have some, Eva dear, won't you?"

Marie laughed, "So you mean all the chickens vill go free from their cages at the same time as Hegley is locked up! Now that *is* justice!"

***

After the meal, Eva carried in a plate of fragrant, hot buns. *"Mazanec!"* she announced proudly.

"Hot cross buns!" everyone chorused. Mr Kleček poured mugs of tea and a satisfied air spread round the room.

Marie felt full and very tired. But something was still puzzling her. She leaned towards Donald. "Can I ask again... about your stick...?"

"Ah yes. I left rather a lot out when you asked me before." Donald wiped his mouth and bent forward. "I usually try to put the past behind me. But these things catch up with you in the end." He stood up and limped over to the wall where his stick rested. Reassured by the feel of it in his hands, he sat down again and began.

"When Dirk came along, I was eight and my parents, who were growing older, were surprised and pleased. To celebrate, my father carved the sticks from a long branch of ash that had come down in a storm the previous winter. We were to have one each when we reached eighteen. I was overjoyed, too: a little brother to play with! Dirk cried like a normal baby, learned to crawl and above all, he grew – taking on the giants on my father's side of the family. There were many hot summers when we splashed in the rivers and ate the whinberries that grew on the wild Mynd."

Marie closed her eyes. It sounded rather like her and Jan. And Shropshire was a special, magic place where nature still had a chance.

"But it was the baby trout that gave me my first clue," Donald continued. "Tricky little flickers of light, they are. Caught them with our nets and put them in a bucket. Only one time, I turned my back, and Dirk had emptied the bucket in the grass and was watching the tiddler flopping around gasping for breath. I thought he was only playing, but the smile on his face worried me. Later, I had an air-gun and was soon an expert at shooting tin cans off walls. But the moment my brother worked out how to aim that thing, no pigeon, crow or jackdaw was safe from his sights. My father tried to explain about respect for wildlife but as Dirk grew older, he fell in with a different gang who had no time for his serious older brother."

Marie looked quickly at Jan and Will and turned away.

"By that time, my parents had no control over him. There were rumours of badger-baiting and even dog-fights. Our lives moved in different directions and I began to feel I'd lost my brother altogether. I got on with my own life, found a job and then was blessed by meeting a girl who was... well... special. 'My treasure', I called her: Charlotte Burne – a local girl who liked nothing better than tramping the hills and getting lost in the borderlands. It seemed perfect, until we bumped into my brother one afternoon. You wouldn't know it now, but when he was young he was as handsome as the devil and had the devil's charm about him. He introduced himself to Charlotte."

Donald paused to take a sip from his tea.

"How could we come of the same stock and yet be so different? My brother saw what made me happy, and determined to have it all for himself. Dirk has hypnotic eyes – you've all seen the effect?" Jan and Marie nodded. "Well, the hunter had her in his sights. And she was young and impressionable…"

"So she…" Marie couldn't believe it.

"Left me for him? Yes. They married, though my parents refused to attend the wedding, and they were right too. Once he'd got her, he quickly grew bored and Charlotte soon found out what sort of man he really was. She realised how stupid she'd been. She walked out on him, but by then it was too late for the two of us. After that, I sort of… turned to the other love of my life – the peregrine." Donald attempted a smile. "Yes, she's a grand beauty, she is! Who knows, maybe when Dirk had an offer to work for Hegley, it was another way of getting back at me…We haven't spoken in thirty-five years!"

"But don't forget, Donald. Your father's stick came to the rescue in the end!" Lady Beddoes said.

"Yes. Surprised myself there. There's life in the old boy yet!" He stared at the carved bird and Jan was sure he saw Donald give it a wink. "Oh, and by the way,

Marie, I don't think that Cassie will be bothering you any more. When Hegley divorced, it was only his money that got him custody of his daughter. The ex-Mrs Hegley has her feet planted firmly on the ground and I know for a fact she won't stand for any nonsense from her daughter."

Mr Kleček raised his glass: "As we Czechs say – please join in – "*Živio!* To Life!" And that is exactly what we are celebrating! *Živio! Živio! Živio!*"

Each time they repeated the word, everyone sang it louder and louder, until Marie was sure the whole of Priestcastle knew that justice had been well and truly done.

New life

It was the middle of May and already the quarry looked different. The trees surrounding the cliffs were weighed with blossom and the chill that had greeted them back in April had been replaced by a thick warmth that smelt of honeysuckle and all things green. Donald led them through the same strange mud-mountain landscape to the tall walls of stone that towered over them and cast early evening shadows. But the smile on Donald's face told another story.

"Here we are." He stopped in the middle of the old track that wound into the centre of the quarry and began setting up his tripod.

"You haven't told us anything yet!" Marie complained.

"That's because I want you to see them with your own eyes!" Donald adjusted the focus, humming to himself. "That's it... yes. Oh good. Now, who's first?"

Doug was the biggest and his natural instinct was to push in front. He turned to Marie. "Go on, then," he grunted.

Marie leaned towards the telescope and put her eye

to the lens. "I can't see anything. It blurs…!"

"Here, adjust the focus on the side."

The scope zoomed in on a ledge in the cliff a hundred metres ahead of them. "Much grass. I can't… oh, I see her!" It was her old friend the peregrine. "There are lots of little grey and white feathers scattered around."

"Pigeon feathers from their last meal, no doubt," said Donald.

"Vot's that?" Marie had spotted a tiny white head bob above the grass, then another and another. "Oh. *To je krásný!*"

Jan was impatient. "What's she looking at? I want to see!"

"Wait!" said Will, "she's the youngest! Let her finish."

Marie could see their little beaks opening and closing.

"I've heard them described as balls of fluff with claws!" said Donald.

"Yes, pure vhite colour. So pretty! Here, you look." She gestured to Jan.

Jan bent over and gasped. "Wow. That is… amazing. They are so tiny. Hang on a second… yeuchhhh! She's tearing off bits of a dead pigeon and… the chicks are grabbing them…" Jan stood back for Doug to look, then Will.

"Well, they do have to eat, you know!" Donald smiled. "After the last theft, the volunteers kept hoping to see this pair mate again. Thank goodness these falcons didn't give up so easily. Sometimes they just desert the scrape for good. But here we are. The chicks hatched over a week ago and a clutch of three is the best news we've had all year!"

"Pretty cool!" admitted Doug. "Hey, what's that?"

They saw a lone magpie swooping down on to the ledge and landing right by the dead pigeon.

"The cheeky imp!" said Donald. "They'll try anything!"

Within seconds, the quarry echoed with cry and counter-cry as the peregrine and magpie screeched and mewed. The smaller peregrine male appeared as a dot in the sky and determinedly pulled in his wings to stoop down and harry the feathered thief. The magpie squawked in annoyance, but accepted that pigeon was not to be on the menu. It took off from the ledge, pursued at full speed by the male.

"Even when they hatch, there are so many dangers," sighed Donald. "If the female leaves the scrape for too long, the jackdaws will happily see those cuddly chicks as tasty breakfast morsels. Then there are foxes, crows, humans or even a big storm that can take the fledglings. But in a few weeks, they'll be able to fly and get away if danger comes."

Donald slowly packed away the telescope. "Thankfully, this lot are in with a good chance, although I do pity the poor male."

"Vhy is that?" asked Marie.

"Looking at the size of them, I'd say that those three chicks are female. In a few weeks he'll not only be outnumbered, but with three sets of bigger claws, he'll be doing his best to avoid the nest!"

"You mean – the female is superior?" said Marie

"Egg-sactly!" smiled Donald.

Marie thumbed her nose at the three boys. Jan tried to trip her over but she hopped deftly out of the way.

"Well, that's that, then," said Donald, "Except for one little thing. I spoke to the Royal Society for the Protection of Birds. Your story is going to be written up in their magazine and you're each going to get a medal…"

The boys looked at each other but didn't seem overly impressed. Doug kicked his heels.

Donald continued, "...and also… that reward!" Now he had their attention. now. "It's going to be split four ways – which I think is fair, don't you?"

Doug grinned. "Not bad!"

"I can get my Ipod!" Jan beamed.

"And I get to keep my treasure safe and sound!" said Donald, looking towards the nest. "Now, I think we could elect you four as honorary members of the Peregrine Watch. What do you say?"

Even Doug nodded enthusiastically. "I often come to the quarry. It won't be much sweat to keep an eye out. It might even keep me out of trouble...!"

"You're not in any rush to get back, are you?" Donald opened his backpack and what he pulled out made a convincing argument for hanging around. "Hot, sweet tea and a delicious lemon cake with eggs from some of Mrs Kleček's *happy* chickens."

The children sat on the rocks and tucked in. As Marie sipped her tea, she felt more than happy to trust in her dreams, particularly as they now featured a decent mountain bike for exploring the hills. What was more, Lady Beddoes' plan to buy the Poultry Palace and transform it was already well under way. So it seemed that these particular dreams were becoming real.

High overhead, swallows dipped and dived and shadows stretched sideways. Everyone gazed up as Donald raised his stick, pointing above the furthest cliff wall. "Anyone would think they were putting on a display just for us!" he whispered.

Five sets of eyes watched in silence as the male peregrine swooped, curving down towards the scrape like an arrow. And as he dropped, the female rose up. They hung in the air for a moment, perfectly balanced, while the sun slowly rolled down behind the far hills.

"Awesome!" Doug breathed, "Makes you feel like... I dunno, like the world just held its breath or something... What? Why are you all looking at me like that?"

The children had lowered their gaze to Doug and were smiling at him.

"What you all smiling at? You laughing at me, or what?"

"Phew. That's more like it!" Will said, "For a moment there, Doug, we thought you were going all poetic on us!"

Doug grinned back, "I don't reckon anyone's called me poetic before and got away with it! But what's wrong with a bit of hope? We all need hope – right?"

"Couldn't agree with you more," said Donald. "Doug, my boy, you have hidden depths! But right now, I'm hoping to get you lot home on time. Come on."

The sky glowed pink and orange behind them as they stumbled away from the quarry.

"You know, I think that this little falcon family are going to turn out just fine," Jan said. Everyone stopped and looked back towards the darkening shape of the ledge as the falcons settled down.

Somehow, it was impossible not to agree.

Czech pronunciation

The language of Czech is filled with quirky pronunciation. Even the word *Czech* is pronounced 'Check'. We put accents on the top of letters which change their sound. The Czech name *Kleček* is pronounced 'Klechek', with a *ch* sound as in 'chat'. The accent ˇ also changes the sound of the letter *s* to *sh*, so *František* is pronounced 'Frantishek'. The letter *c* in the middle or at the end of words is often pronounced with a *ts* sound. *Jan* is pronounced with a *y* to become 'Yan', and *Marie* is pronounced 'Marry', with a slight roll on the *r*.

We are also proud to have one of the most difficult-to-pronounce sounds in the world. It occurs in the family name of our famous composer Antonín Dvořák. The accent above the *r* changes the sound into a partly-rolled *rr* followed by a softened *dge* sound with a hint of *z* in it. It's very difficult to describe – easier when you say it!

Czech Glossary
(pronunciation in italics)

Ano! To jsou ty vajíčka *(Ano! Toe yi-sow ty vy-yeech-kaa)*: These are the eggs

Ahoj *(A-hoy)*: hello

Co se stalo? *(Co se sta-lo)*: What happened?

Dobrou chut! *(Doo-brow chut)*: Bon appetit!

Fantastický! *(Fan-tas-tit-skee)*: fantastic!

Sakra! *(Sak-ra)*: Damn!

Janíčku *(Ya-neech-ku)*: Jan (affectionate)

Maruško *(Ma-rroosh-ko)*: Marie (affectionate)

mazanec *(mu-zu-netc)*: hot cross bun

Táto *(Tah-to)*: Dad

To je krásný *(To ye kraas-nee)*: It is beautiful.

Živio! *(Zhiv-yo)*: To life!

Andrew Fusek Peters and **Polly Peters**
are the authors of over 55 books for children and
teenagers, among them the first in the Czech Mate
series, *Roar, Bull, Roar!* This was shortlisted for the
Stockport Schools Award. Their most recent teenage
novel, *Crash*, was nominated for the Carnegie Medal,
shortlisted for the North East Book Award and
described as "original to its core – it should be read
in classrooms up and down the land" – *Times
Educational Supplement*. Andrew's family fled from
Prague in 1948 during the communist coup, bringing
with them only stories. He has been visiting schools
and festivals since 1987 with his poetry, tales and
didgeridoo. Polly is a former teacher. Andrew
and Polly live in Shropshire with their children
and a bored goldfish.

Find out more at www.tallpoet.com

Roar, Bull, Roar!

Andrew Fusek Peters and Polly Peters
Illustrated by Anke Weckmann

Czech brother and sister Jan and Marie arrive
in rural England – and not everyone is welcoming.
As they try to settle into their new school, they are
plunged into a series of mysteries. Old legends are
revived as they unearth shady secrets in a desperate
bid to save their family from eviction.

*A fast moving adventure story... Children will relish
the humour and pace of the tale as it speeds up to its
dramatic climax involving lost children, wicked deeds,
car chases and a splendidly eccentric bullfight
in the deep winter snow.* School Librarian

An enjoyable and exciting read. CBUK

ISBN 978-1-84507-520-0

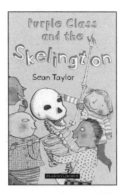

Purple Class and the Skelington

Sean Taylor
Illustrated by Helen Bate
Cover illustrated by Polly Dunbar

Meet Purple Class – there is Jamal who often
forgets his reading book, Ivette who is the best in
the class at everything, Yasmin who is sick on every
school trip, Jodie who owns a crazy snake called
Slinkypants, Leon who is great at rope-swinging,
Shea who knows all about blood-sucking slugs
and Zina who makes a rather disturbing
discovery in the teacher's chair...

ISBN: 978-1-84507-377-0

Butter-Finger

Bob Cattell and John Agard
Illustrated by Pam Smy

Riccardo Small may not be a great cricketer –
he's only played twice before for Calypso Cricket Club –
but he's mad about the game and can tell you the
averages of every West Indies cricketer in history.
His other love is writing calypsos. Today is Riccardo's
chance to make his mark with Calypso CC against
The Saints. The game goes right down to the wire
with captain, Natty and team-mates, Bashy and Leo
striving for victory, but then comes the moment
that changes everything for Riccardo…

ISBN 978-1-84507-376-3